The Madonnina

The Madonnina

BERND SCHROEDER

Translated from the German by Anthea Bell

Weidenfeld & Nicolson
LONDON

First published in Germany in 2001 by Carl Hanser Verlag as *Die Madonnina*

First published in Great Britain in 2004 by Weidenfeld and Nicolson

A CIP catalogue record for this book is
available from the British Library.

ISBN 0 297 82986 6

Typeset by Deltatype Ltd,
Birkenhead, Merseyside

Printed in Great Britain by
Clays Ltd, St Ives plc

Weidenfeld and Nicolson
The Orion Publishing Group Ltd
Orion House
5 Upper Saint Martin's Lane
London, WC2H 9EA

For Elena

I

Severina will never again forget that face. A face in which all the malice and stupidity, all the arrogance and presumption of which a human being is capable are united. The face of the young carabiniere at the police station down in the valley.

2

The crooked, intricately twining branches of the bushes, hardly as high as a man and with nothing above them but sparse grass giving way to rocks, are tenaciously alive and set themselves to thwart Severina. The branches have crept along the ground as they grew, intertwining again and again, always dipping down once more; no sooner have they grown than they turn back to the earth, as if overawed by the sight of the sky stretching so close above them. Parts of them are as thick as Severina's upper arm, they spring back, creaking, they defend themselves, evade her, whip back, strike at her, coming into the front line one by one; they scratch her, grudging every blow of her well-sharpened knife. But she knows that if they resist her like that, it means they will last a long time when they go up in flames on the hearth later. They sing in the fire, especially when they are not quite dry, they sing eerie songs, bringing up from within them the music of long, lonely winter evenings up here in the mountains.

Severina's back is aching. She slashes at the tangle of branches with the shining blade again and again, finally pulls a very crooked, distorted branch out and throws it down the slope behind her to join the others. This job often seems the hardest work of all, and may be pointless, because she is cutting wood to keep her warm the winter after next. Will she still be here then?

She is sweating. The sun burns pitilessly down on her, without a cloud to trouble it. She decides to stop now and go on later in the afternoon, when the sun has disappeared behind the peak of the Madonnina. She stands up, for she has been kneeling down to work, she stretches, bends her back, puts one hand to a painful spot in the small of it, and feels a little dizzy. The mountain tops, standing out brownish-yellow against the blue sky, seem to be moving, coming closer and then retreating. She gazes at a rent in the sky, a white line, using it to get her bearings before it dissolves and merges into the heavens. The familiar contours of the foothills of the mountains, with the path nestling close to them as it winds half-way up to the farm, the silvery-white trees in the yard, pale and bony skeletons in winter, become sharper again, then abruptly quiver once more for a fraction of a second. A shrill note, a whirring cry like the sound of an arrow shot from the bow, resounds through the valley, rises up the hills, breaks among the bushes, shatters on rock. It is followed by silence, a silence that exists only because it was preceded by that note. For a fraction of a second the world holds its breath.

Someone has struck the cable. Someone is coming, has announced his arrival by hitting the cable, someone who doesn't want to turn up without warning, and has just given notice that he will be here in about half an hour's time.

Who will it be? The faithful and kindly Franco-Francone, hauling his girth uphill to make sure that she and the old woman are all right? Her father, come to try persuading her to go back to the village? Her brothers, that impatient, quick-tempered couple, sent by their father? Or Sebastiano, who sometimes guides tourists up to the peak of the Madonnina? Severina looks over to the place where the path disappears for the last time behind a hill before plunging down to the valley. She should soon get a brief glimpse there of whoever is coming, a small moving dot recognisable from where she stands only if you are very familiar with his walk, his bearing, his stature, his way of moving. Severina knows who is coming at once.

It's not Franco-Francone, whose weight makes him waddle, so that he seems to be in danger of falling into the abyss any time he puts a foot wrong. Her brothers wouldn't come up separately, and her father walks more laboriously, more slowly, with deliberation. Sebastiano would be surrounded by tourists tripping lightly along. No, the new arrival has a sure, firm tread, knows every centimetre of the path, skilfully avoids small obstacles over which he might stumble, walks with a spring in his step, strides purposefully along, faster than anyone else she knows. Then he disappears again behind the next hill.

It's him.

3

It's him. She can sense it. She can see it. She can see it very clearly. It's him. He's the only man who walks like that, no one else moves in the same way. That's how he always came up from the village below, that's how she always recognised him in the distance, even before he struck the cable to say he was coming. That was how he climbed the mountains even in winter, to chop wood with Franco-Francone and Bruno and the others, that was how he walked through the village too, admired openly or secretly by the women chatting and giggling together as they stood at the wash-tubs, or hiding their dreams behind the net curtains of their living-rooms, their hearts beating fast.

He is the only man who walks like that. And that was how, a year ago, he climbed to the peak of the Madonnina, the mountain that takes its name from the Madonnina on Milan Cathedral. On a clear day you can see her from the top of the mountain. With a light but sure tread, drawing that fluttering, giggling, over-exuberant, inebriated party of tourists along behind him as if on an invisible string, the only woman among them close on his heels, a gaudy, half-plucked chicken of a woman accompanied by four thin figures, puppets carved from spindly branches, their dark city suits hanging loose on them. They looked like crows stalking along. A ludicrous sight, a funeral procession for a parrot, the witch queen with her silly court climbing a mountain. An image like something out of a picture-book, at once ridiculous, fascinating and disturbing. Massimo leading the way, their guide, hired as so often by tourists down in the bar. The others followed him, tripping clumsily in their light summer shoes, always fearing to fall into the abyss, dancing mincingly, foolishly after him as he strode powerfully along, and towards the end of the path, where it climbs steeply, he carried the young woman up piggy-back, concerned solely for her. Severina's gaze followed him until he disappeared in the mist at the top of the peak. Gone for ever, was the thought that shot through her head, gone for a long time anyway, far longer than that day, a day when, as Severina kept telling herself afterwards for comfort, you couldn't see the Madonnina, who was really a larger-than-life Madonna, you couldn't see the Madonnina at all.

You could see the Madonnina today.

4

Massimo has reached the top station of the transport cableway after about half an hour's climb; it takes him no longer. From here the path snakes along the slopes in many winding curves, a narrow path meant for sheep and goats, but it serves the herdsmen too. He is breathing harder than he remembers doing. It was a tougher climb than usual because he's out of practice. He has spent too long walking down level streets, along narrow, noisy alleys full of people, with a dirty sky above. The guide wheel above the cable is rusty, and so is the winch. Grass has grown into the drive system, a twining plant has wound its way into the beginning of the cable and crept along it, as if to strangle it by suffocation. It is a long time since anything was transported along the cableway. The iron bar you used to strike it, as a signal that the load was ready to go or to announce that you would be there yourself in half an hour, is still lying beside the winch. Massimo strikes the cable briefly, hard and with all his might. It groans, shivers, a quivering ripple runs all the way along its length, and it makes a high, whirring note that threatens to crack the blue glass bell of the air above the mountains. Massimo looks up, follows the whirring sound as it shatters against the rocks, and sees nothing in the sky but a long white rent rapidly merging into the blue.

Now she'll know he's coming. She is familiar with his way

of making that sound. She will see him from the farm and know him by the way he walks. What will happen when they are face to face? Will some other man come out to meet him and ask what he's doing here, while she hides in the background, in the dim light of the shed or behind the glass of the window-panes, staring silently at him? If there's no other man here who has taken his place, will she shout, rage, scream at him, call him names, say he's a bastard and a coward? Yes, she will, no doubt about it. There won't be another man there rapidly doing up his trousers and shirt before facing the husband whose reappearance he has long feared, whose slippers he has worn, whose wine he drinks, whose work he does, whose bed and wife he has taken over. No, there will be no other man there, she'll be alone with her anger, the anger of her long wait for him, an anger fed by the silent reproaches of the old woman, his mother, whose love he can count on as he always could. Yes, that's what he will wish for, that's how it should be. He was always able to deal with her anger; it just flowed off him like water off a duck's back. He used to hunch his head between his shoulders, not looking at her, working in silence, waiting for her to run out of words. No, he isn't afraid of her loud and angry accusations. But then she knows that too. Massimo begins to be afraid she may keep silent instead, say nothing, simply remain mute.

She's not talking these days.

Rosanna said.

What does a woman do with her anger if she doesn't speak, if she doesn't shout and scream? What would silent anger be like? He has always felt uneasy with people who kept quiet instead of quarrelling, answering back, arguing. He feared them, feeling that they were on top of him, sitting on his shoulders, urging him on with a whip. It was when she, that other woman in her own bed there, stopped screaming at him, stopped shouting, raging and cursing and instead fell silent, merely looking at him with silent contempt, that he knew his time was up and he must go. And so he had left, he had gone back to the railway station again, where he had been several times before, but this time no desire held him back. Instead, it was another, vaguely felt and still ill-defined yearning that made him board the train.

5

He really wanted to stay down in the village house and not come up until tomorrow or the day after, returning slowly and cautiously, coming back to the village first and letting rumour go on ahead of him. When he got off the bus in the square under the plane trees, peaceful at noon, with the bowling alley lying at rest, he said goodbye to talkative Luigi who had now turned so melancholy and went into Teresa's bar, where she greeted him with an: Oh, here you are again!, as if he had been away for just a day or so, not a whole year. Yet there was curiosity in her casual manner of putting down his glass of wine, with a soft coo of: Well? She wanted the privilege of being the first to hear his story, and she wanted to tell him theirs. But he left her in suspense, punishing her by acting as if he really had just been paying a brief visit to town. So her second: Well? was more of a sigh, because what was she going to say when everyone asked her questions that evening? Massimo drained his glass, shouldered his bundle and left. Teresa decided to think up some excuse to look in on Rosanna that afternoon, for Rosanna would surely manage to get more out of him. After all, if Rosanna was to be believed, she had repeatedly dragged him into her bed full of dolls. Yes, she'd question Rosanna, and her own imagination would supply the rest. But you did need a few clues. After all, nobody knew anything much for sure. There was nothing definite, nothing certain, nothing from any authoritative source, only rumours which could hardly be checked for veracity. The old woman up there, his mother, said he was in Germany, other people claimed to have seen him in a pizzeria in Milan, and even worse things were whispered: some said he was a pimp in a brothel these days. No one knew the truth of it. Hadn't he arrived with Luigi, hadn't they travelled by bus together, presumably all the way along the lake from Como to Menaggio, then through the villages and up here? Mightn't it be a good idea to question Luigi? But would he tell her anything true, credible, guaranteed authentic and worth passing on? In the past, before Luigi turned so melancholy, it would all have come pouring out of him, oh yes. But now he would just keep his mouth shut and go his own way. So no one knew anything. They'd have to wait and keep their ears pricked. One thing Teresa must say, however: Massimo had always wanted to be something special, he was always on the look-out for strangers, always wanted to know more about them than anyone else here did. Then along came that woman, the woman from Milan with her four companions. And next thing you knew, Severina was searching for him in a panic, but he'd gone, run off with that woman. That woman – oh yes, he could sometimes sweet-talk women, tell them things, listen to them, and he could dance with them too, exchanging soulful glances, showing that he liked their company. And they liked his. Yes, there was that too.

Massimo went up the street to the house, and he saw at first glance that she hadn't been here, hadn't been living in the place, had not come down in autumn to spend the winter there. The gate squealed and was overgrown with twining plants, like the fence, the front garden had run wild, was full of thistles, and the grass was already knee-high between the paving stones. Then, as if she had been lurking behind the net curtains in her kitchen for the whole of the last year, just waiting for this moment, Rosanna immediately appeared, and her voice held all the derision stoked up by her long wait.

There, you can see for yourself.

See what?

She's let the place go to rack and ruin.

Yes, I see that.

What you see there – ha, as if what you saw at first glance was the whole story!

Then I'll soon find out the rest of it.

I could tell you a thing or two!

Go on, then, tell them!

I said, I could tell you a thing or two.

Or don't, just as you please.

She came here twice. The last time was in autumn, all by herself, in secret. She crept down in the dark like a thief. Like a thief, hear that? Groping her way around the house, her own house, like a thief! Didn't want to be seen, wanted to make out she hadn't been there at all. But I saw her!

Because you see everything, don't you?

I saw her.

You see everything, you see what's none of your business. You see that too. You see it first.

Ha, ha, none of my business? So that's how you view it!

What there once was between us – I've forgotten and you certainly ought to forget it too ... Well, it gives you no right. Not to anything.

She didn't even put a light on. But I saw her. I went over, tapped on the window. She'd flung herself down on the floor. Lying there like the dead. I tapped again and rattled the door. I called out to her, but she just lay there like the dead. Then she went up to the bedroom, brought the bedclothes down and put them in the hearth. The bedclothes off the bed. You know, the bed up there.

I know.

She put them in the hearth and set fire to them. And I saw her face in the firelight. Oh, Jesus and Mary! I could certainly tell you!

Tell me what?

Mad.

Mad?

She'd gone mad. Stark staring mad.

Well, well.

What do you mean, well, well?

It'll all be different now.

Now?

Now I'm back.

Now you're back? Ha, ha!

Yes. It will all be different, it'll be the way it used to be.

You mean because you're back?

Yes.

Ha, ha!

He left her standing there, eager as she was to dig a knife deeper and deeper into the wound, find a bullet to shoot him with if things weren't to be the way they used to be between him and her, if he wasn't going to slip into her bed full of dolls with her any more and make her feel, briefly, that someone needed her, someone wanted her. She'd got accustomed to that feeling, and she missed it so much that she had thought recently, more and more often, that she couldn't bear her dreary life any more.

No, it wasn't to her he had come back. Not that, not now. He went into the house. He was met by a musty smell, the usual musty smell of the house when they came down to it in winter after spending the summer in the mountains, when the mice and spiders had claimed the place for themselves.

Yet this mustiness in the house was not all. Severina's jealous and desperate work of destruction was clear to see, accusing him, throwing his guilt in his face, and it was accompanied by the triumph of Rosanna, following him closer than he liked, with that aroma about her of the yellow liqueur on her bedside table, with her white flesh, her powder, the knowledge of her lustful lair up there in the bed, the barely controlled, barely concealed desire that cried silently out of her.

There, you see? You can see it for yourself, look. She came down like an avenging angel. She went everywhere, saw everyone. And everyone laughed at her, she went to see the carabinieri, then along all the roads, into the fields, into kitchens, into the wash-house and the church, the fire station and Angelo's butcher's shop, she was chasing around like a mad thing, asking questions and shouting your name. She went to the graveyard, stood and called to you by the grave of your baby who died, trying to conjure you up. And later she came down here once again, came all the way down in secret like a thief in the night, like a thief!

He could see it all.

You see?

He saw. He saw the half-burnt bedclothes in the hearth, the champagne bottles that had been thrown at the wall, all that was left of that drunken spree, the contents of the kitchen cupboard scattered on the floor, the pictures of hunting scenes torn off the wall, the china smashed to bits on the mildewed floor which had probably swollen up when a tap was deliberately turned on to flood it.

There, you can see for yourself.

He did. Upstairs, he saw the mattress of the double bed slit open with a knife, the wedding photo trampled underfoot, trodden on the floor, two faces fragmented like pieces of a jigsaw puzzle. He saw the images of furious destruction that had followed his own misuse of the house that night. Rosanna was trying to kindle rage in him, and he was looking for it in himself too, but he couldn't find any. Instead he felt the warmth of pride, a feeling that, at this moment, seemed like desire. She had tried to destroy everything they had in common, she had overturned their love and their life together because he had gone. Had that woman in the city so much as torn up one of her pretty cushions when he said he was finally leaving? No. She had smoked, lying back on the cushions half-naked, letting her body alone say: Stay if you like. But the words that came out of her mouth were coarse: Fuck off if you like, then!

So he had gone, and come back, and gone again, for her mouth had suddenly fallen silent.

Rosanna sensed what was passing through his mind. She saw no anger in his face, only a slight, dreamy smile instead, and she didn't know which of his possible reactions seemed more likely to promote her personal interest in getting her lover back.

You see how it was. She went mad because you went away with that – that –

With that what? Oh, be quiet.

That person.

That person? What do you mean? Don't talk about someone when you know nothing about her.

I know what I see, and that's the truth. And I remember what I've seen.

So what do you think you saw that was the truth?

I saw you that time. I saw you with that person. I saw you lose your head over her. That's what I saw.

Ah, did you, though?

So now you're back.

Can't you see that, when you see everything else?

How long for?

What's that to do with you?

He ran downstairs, not wanting to see it any more, the mattress slit open, just wanting to leave, to go up the mountain to her now. And Rosanna ran after him, wanting at least, in the sad desperation of her life, to know if a little part of him had come back for her too, just a little of what had always been hers and had been enough for her.

For her small, greedy, vengeful triumph had long since given way to fear and despair. She stood at the door with tears in her eyes, as if she could stop him, bar his way, keep him there for her bed full of dolls upstairs. If there was one thing Massimo could do without just now, it was tears that were not tears of joy at the moment of reunion. He didn't look at her, didn't see her face dissolve in despair, didn't see or even feel the desire that was destroying her, and the whole edifice of her hunger for love and her curiosity.

And are you going to stay?

I expect so.

Aha.

Yes.

And everything will be the way it used to be?

No. Nothing will be the way it used to be.

How else will it be, then, now you're back?

Different.

Huh!

Very different.

Huh! You'll go up there and it will be the way it used to be. And you'll come down and go to the bar, and after that you'll be too tired to go up again, and you'll be cold in here, and you'll see a light in my house, I'll put a candle in the window specially for you, and you'll want me and that will bring you over here. You'll say come on, Rosanna, come up to your bed with those thousand dolls, and you'll throw all the dolls on the floor and want me, all of me, me and my body. And then –

And then, and then – what then?

And then it will be the way it used to be.

He knew himself too well to be able to deny it entirely. But at the moment he didn't want to be in the arms she so willingly reached out to him. No. He would go up the mountain now, carry all his guilt up to her, take his place beside her again, be there for her, live with the mountain again, with the animals, the farm, the people up above and here in the valley, and with her. Then he might return to Rosanna's bed at night now and then, the bed that her husband Paolo, who lived and worked in Switzerland during the week, claimed only at weekends. And then he was usually drunk.

Rosanna felt she couldn't keep him now, not even for a swift reunion in her bed, and since she felt a little afraid that he might have changed after all over the last year, might have become used to something other than her and her body, might despise her, she played the last trump card she still held.

So you're going up to see that mute woman today, are you?

Mute?

Yes, mute.

What do you mean, mute?

She isn't talking these days.

Not talking?

No.

Why not?

Why not, why not?

Since when?

Since she realised you'd gone away with that person, since she went all over the place trying to find you. She went to the carabinieri too, you know. She hasn't spoken a word since then.

Not to anyone?

No. Not to Franco-Francone, or Bruno and Paolo, or any of the other men, or even her brothers and her father, and she hasn't spoken to your old mother either.

Massimo stared at Rosanna. How she was enjoying being the first to give him this news! She felt a glimmer of hope that she might keep him from going up there. If she's mad, he'd say, what would I want with her?

Rosanna added fuel to the flames.

Her father and brothers went up there at the time. They lashed out at her, she didn't utter a sound, she was like a woman with her tongue cut out.

Is this true?

Massimo, she's mad, crazy!

God in heaven.

She hits the old woman. She stayed up there all winter. With the animals. Your mother almost froze to death.

He was getting restless, nothing would keep him here now, and these words, which seemed to be concealing the greed, jealousy, desire and all the wretchedness of Rosanna's life, reached him only from a distance. He locked up the house, waved briefly to Rosanna and prepared to set out. She held him back for a moment, pressing hungrily against him and whispering to him, although there was no one to hear her.

The dolls, Massimo, you always said my dolls were in your way. I've got rid of them all.

He shook himself free and left.

Energetically, longingly, quickening his pace, gaining height and freer air, he strode away up the mountain along the familiar narrow path.

And Rosanna returned to her coloured bottles on the

mantelpiece, the liqueurs that were more and more of a comfort to her.

That afternoon Teresa looked in.

Massimo's back.

I know.

Well?

He's back.

Yes, go on, tell me about it!

6

Here he comes. She sees him come into view and then disappear again. It's him, yes, no doubt about it. And he's announced his arrival, has told her: I'm coming. He could have come up without striking the cable. He could have come up, just appeared here. He could have taken her by surprise, exploiting her helplessness and inability to deal with such a situation. But he never did that. She always had time to prepare for him in between the moment when he struck the cable and the moment of his arrival, time to feel alarmed or glad, to assume an appropriate expression one way or the other. She has not used the cableway since he left. Franco-Francone has brought her up the necessities of life. He will have seen at once that the cable hasn't been used. Grass will have grown into it, it will be rusty; she no longer wanted that steely link with the world down below.

He struck the cable. She immediately recognised the high-pitched, whirring, unmistakable note that brought her out of the deepest of dreams. He struck the cable, giving her time as he always did, and she liked that. But time for what now? Time to run off and hide? Time to collect her thoughts, pull herself together, go to meet him with a firm: What are you doing here? Time to run and meet him with a: So here you are at last? What does she feel now, at this moment, as he grows larger and comes closer with every bend in the path?

What's inside her? Anxiety, apprehension, anger, joy? Joy? Yes. She is startled, for it is joy that now makes her heart beat faster, a joy which she feared in the lonely nights, with no company but the rustle of the silvery leaves of the trees in the yard. This joy now threatens to sweep aside all the desperation of the past year. No, it must not. The suffering, the silence, the isolation she has created around her, her refusal to speak, her silent war with the old woman, the cold nights, her desires, her memories of better times and her secret hopes – they must not be shattered by his cheerful: Here I am again!, like a soap bubble when your finger touches it, bursting into a void, as if nothing had happened. No. He can't simply come back as if it had never been, as if she had never paid her humiliating visit to the carabinieri. There's no place now at the table for a man who just comes back after a year to sit down, drink wine, eat bread and salami, throw the leftovers into the fire, tell stories of life down below, laugh at her credulity, pass his hard, rough-skinned hand over her face, draw her towards him. No. There's nothing to sit on but the bench beside the fire for the old woman and her chair. She burned the other one for fuel in the winter. She didn't need it any more. Oh, how the old woman shrieked, what a fuss she made! It was nothing to do with her, for when she turned mute she also became deaf to what she didn't want to hear. If you don't have to answer because you never speak, then you needn't show that you hear what is being said.

Oh, if only there was a man here now to walk out and meet him with a determined step, with all the rights of a man who was now slaughtering the farm chickens, cutting the wood, shearing the sheep, bringing up wine and provisions from the village, repairing the roof of the shed! Someone to ask him: What are you doing here, who are you, why are you bringing your stranger's face up here to disturb our peace?

Even if it was Franco-Francone, that three-hundredweight overgrown child, who was always dragging himself up here to express his sweaty and unreasonable desire for her body. Franco-Francone would oppose him with his great belly, would be a bulwark, would crush him, squeeze all his lying deception out of his guts, so that he'd have to escape down to the valley, to general derision.

Oh, Franco-Francone, why didn't I listen when you tried putting that crumpled little thing of yours in my hand? Why didn't I give in to your babyish pleas at least once, your hot panting, your greed, your damp fingers groping me, your tongue heavy with red wine licking my hand like a dog's, why didn't I take you just once, give you release from your whimpering and wailing, so that now you'd be a tower of strength, an impenetrable fence to me?

But yes, Franco-Francone, I know he'd stand in front of you, put his strong, sunburnt, hairy hand on your shoulder, look at you with his bright eyes under those thick black brows, smile the smile which has always brought him everything he wanted in life, saying: Hello there, Franco-Francone, old friend, old comrade, glad to see you've been looking after her. And then you would weep your tears of emotion, tears for a man, a friend, a comrade, a fellow hunter, the clear, honest tears of loyalty, man to man, not the sweaty tears of disappointment you wept over me. And you'd fall into his arms with a guilty conscience, asking him to forgive you, keeping your friend, the friend you need more than any brief, rapid moaning over me and my body, overstraining your heart and your powers of imagination.

Severina looks down the valley. She can see him again, she can clearly make out his black hair now. He's coming closer. He's coming. He really is coming back. She is still standing there as if rooted to the ground, at one with the bushes. She wants to move and can't, wants to run away but still stands there, always looking the same way, to where he is disappearing behind a hill that hides the path. He'll be in sight again in a moment, getting larger again, closer again, more menacing again, and there's no one to go out and meet him. No one. No bulwark, no tower of strength, no impenetrable fence, not even a Franco-Francone. Only the trees in the yard, those silent, peaceful, patient witnesses to all that has happened. They say nothing, they do not move, they wait until winter to tell their tales, when they are alone up here with the language of their last frozen autumn leaves in the icy wind.

7

They came back down just as they had gone up. The woman tripping along like an injured bird behind Massimo, who had carried her down the steep part of the slope on his back, and was now striding firmly ahead. Behind them came the boys, dandies, jumping-jacks, carved wooden Pinocchios, frail walking skeletons, complaining, exhausted, and disappointed because they hadn't seen the Madonnina. They were grumbling, but the sound didn't reach Massimo and Renata, who were playing their own game, celebrating a festival together. All the others had moved away, were simply background figures. Complaining, cursing, dozing off, one playing the accordion, another tapping out the rhythm on a wine bottle with spoons, the figures in the background were musical accompaniment. The woman's four companions, the sheep, the goats, the trees, the old woman on the bench outside the house, they were the music to which the two of them danced. Renata jumped up at Massimo, flung her arms round his neck and her legs round his hips and kissed him, all confused as he was, standing there bewildered under the trees with a bottle of wine, her chosen victim. Severina could see all this from the house. She stiffened, trembled, froze, felt all the fears she had heard other women express, fears that had never been hers. Not when he was down in the village and didn't come up until next morning, and she guessed that Rosanna was luring him into her bed with all those countless dolls. Rosanna, Severina knew, could take nothing away from her. Rosanna was just helping herself to a man who, if he weren't available to provide a few happy hours in her sad life, would sleep down in the house in the village, snoring, dreamless, drunk, without a wish or a thought in his head. If anything, it was reassuring when Severina guessed he was with Rosanna and no one else, for Rosanna could be relied upon not to let any other woman get her hands on this occasional and only allegedly secret conquest of hers. No, Severina didn't fear Rosanna. But the woman out there, clucking around her Massimo, tripping about, cooing and sighing, purring and winding him in, hopping, dancing, fluttering, this dream creature from a world unknown to Severina threatened to upset all her well-ordered feelings.

Was she the crazy one, not he? She was standing in the shed now, in the dark, away from the glances of the others out there, looking through the small, murky window. She saw him prancing about, handing round the bottle, courting her, entertaining her, she saw everything that was meant only for the woman she had seen him carrying up to the peak of the Madonnina on his back just a few hours earlier, her breath hot on his throat, her arms round him, her little breasts against his shoulder-blades. She saw him courting this stranger, her looks and her laughter, her freely given kisses, her proximity, her body pressed against him as if by chance. Severina saw all this, and felt in her inmost being that she loved him. She loved him even as he was losing himself, she loved him even as he was moving away from her, she loved him although she knew in advance, before he did, that she was going to lose him to this woman and to these people, to the air of another world. And as so often happened, her feelings took her thoughts by surprise: it was a long time since she had felt so close to him, had longed for him as she did now. Yes, back then, of course, when she was up at the party in Oggia with her sister Anna, shyly looking around her, watching the men and assessing her own market value by their reactions, excited, expectant, intoxicated by the men's part-songs and the seductive melodies of the clarinets, when he was suddenly standing before her, dancing with her again and again all evening, and she saw his bright eyes, loved him immediately, more than she ever loved him again after that. Anyway, their life together had become habit, they took each other for granted just as they did everything, it was always the same, they no longer knew the sudden lust for each other that could tolerate no delay, the chance touch that made you catch fire, the little squeals of delight uttered without a thought for the old woman in the next room.

That was all memory now, only a secret wish, desire in the nights up here when he was down in the valley, desire nourished by the idea that he might be lying with Rosanna now. But now, now that this vulture of misfortune who came flying over the mountains with her company of four black ravens had made him her victim, she loved him as fiercely as the mother cat loves the kitten that a buzzard has just swooped down to snatch up from her. She loved all he was conjuring up over there, she was secretly proud of him, yet she felt a panic that took her voice away, made breathing difficult, caused her to take root here in the shed like a wooden post. Out there Massimo was no longer walking but floating. He kept fetching wine, salami, bread, cheese, all in great abundance, plundering the provisions that had been so laboriously carried up. He laughed at the woman's jokes, which were strange to him, sang her songs, which he didn't know, and finally let her hear those songs of his own that he usually sang only and almost devoutly as part-songs with his friends. It was all betrayal, betrayal by a man now out of his mind. What was this woman to him, this thin, bony goat draped in a few loose scraps of fabric that hid almost nothing, since there wasn't anything much to hide? What did he want from her? What tempted him, he who was the real seducer and had always preferred a sturdy, firm, red-cheeked, well rounded girl, who had wanted her, Severina, and not her beautiful sister Anna? Was it a presentiment of something quite different, something which should really be feared but which he, who was afraid of nothing, did not fear at all but wanted to challenge instead? Was it really much more than this woman that he longed for? Was she only the harbinger of another world, another life? Severina didn't understand any of it. How could she, when she didn't understand him and he, who usually explained everything to her, was now out of his own mind? Now he was standing quite close to her. She withdrew even further into the darkness of the shed. He should really have seen her, smelled her if he had eyes for her, if he had thought of her at all. He was standing by the bird-cage that he had built a couple of years ago. And for the first time Severina heard him call the woman's name. It went through her like an electric shock.

Renata!

Yes?

Come here!

Coming! Coming!

She spoke in fluting tones, whirled round, ran, flew to him, came down half beside and half on him, pressed against him, laid her cheek to his heated face, literally breathed in his words.

Look, do you see them, the birds – all my birds, the birds I've caught?

Yes.

Aren't they lovely?

Oh yes, yes.

At that moment Severina, who now understood everything

and could watch this thin woman's face, smell her perfume, see her shaved armpits, sensed something of the way you can win power over a man by pretending interest, a shared passion, saying what he expects to hear at a given moment.

Yes, lovely, said Renata, in such matter-of-fact and casual tones that if Massimo had been in his right mind he would instantly have seen her lack of interest. But as it was, her words struck him as a charming song, as sympathy with his passion for his birds, and his eyes, troubled by the smell of her, by her body and her breath, rested so happily on the feathered captives that it was unnecessary for the young woman even to look at the birds. She was so sure of herself, as Severina could see. She was the most interesting, the brightest bird he thought he had ever caught.

It had never been Severina's way to show joy or sympathy where she didn't feel it, to pretend to feelings that she did not have. It was beyond her, therefore, that this stranger could claim an interest in the birds, to please Massimo, by uttering a mere: Yes, lovely. Severina was no longer surprised that the woman could do that to him, or what remained of him, for he wasn't himself any more.

She had always hated his passion for trapping and imprisoning the birds, and he knew it. She felt sorry for them. She loved the birds when they circled above the valley, soared up or came down, flew away again from cats and human noises. She had never understood what pleasure he could take in robbing the birds of their freedom, as proud of his catch as if he had shot a hare, sitting in front of the cage to watch their desperate efforts to get through the bars, conquer the open air again, the sky, the trees, the mountain tops. Why did he enjoy that? Is it something a man needs, Severina wondered, the way he needs to go hunting with friends, fishing, fighting, doing military service, brawling? Is he a man only when he can show the animals that he has the power of life or death over them? But weren't her own mother and his mother, the old woman, just the same? They mocked a chicken before cutting off its head, while she, Severina, always apologised to the fowl for what she had to do. She had always refused to feed the poor prisoners in the bird-cage and look after them, even look at them at all. If Massimo wasn't there the old woman did what was necessary. She triumphantly did all she could for her beloved son in Severina's place.

And when he failed to come back after taking that intoxicated, well-fed company down to the valley along with his conquest, when Severina came up again after her vain search, she went to the bird-cage and opened the little door in the wire netting to let the prisoners out into freedom. But they found this offer so unusual, so strange, so confusing that they were as helpless to deal with it as Severina was to deal with what had happened. They did not escape, did not fly away at once, but sat there anxiously as usual, desperately flying into the netting through which they saw trees and sky, sensing freedom. They did not get far. Their little skulls collided with the wire, which sometimes stunned them so that they sat there for a long time trembling or as if dead on the droppings covering the floor. Their wings broke, shredded, lost feathers. If they had managed to reach freedom and tried to fly away, they would have landed ignominiously somewhere in the farmyard, easy pickings for the cats. At some time or other the old woman shut the door in the wire netting again, and from then on Severina regarded these prisoners as her companions in misfortune.

8

Massimo can already see the trees in the farmyard, the house, the stable, the stacked wood, the sheep, the henhouse at the very end of the valley, where there is nothing but rocks and the steep, narrow path up to the peak of the Madonnina. The scene will disappear twice more behind a hill, and he must skirt that hill before it lies ahead of him like a picture hanging on the wall. These little hills, the last rocky hilltops, fissured and only sparsely overgrown, with the blue sky hanging over them close enough to touch, do not offer much protection from the sun, casting small shadows only into the most remote crannies. Massimo is perspiring, panting, breathing hard. This is not how he thinks of himself. He isn't used to climbing mountains any more, he has spent a year on level ground, walking down streets lined by huge buildings, usually with a dirty sky above. The spring of water lies beyond those bushes over there. He reaches it. Now, in summer, it is a trickle finding its way through smooth stones, moss and low-growing plants. Massimo hits the stones with his stick, scrapes his feet and makes a lot of noise to scare away the vipers that like to bask here in the sun near water on hot summer days, deceptively blending into the ground, scarcely visible, indistinguishable from the stones, timid, fleeing from sounds, but dangerous if they attack human beings and usually deadly to sheep.

Massimo's father hated vipers more than anything in the world. They were always killing sheep, particularly the thoughtless lambs who came down to the water. To Massimo as a child, the vipers were the very embodiment of evil spirits. His father would lie in wait for them, often standing motionless for hours, watching the silvery brown reptiles lying in the sand or on stones in the sun, and then striking suddenly, quick as lightning, using a forked branch. Other people killed vipers with a well-aimed blow to the head, but not Massimo's father. The boy had to learn how to catch vipers when he was quite young. You have to get the forked branch round behind the snake's head and press it to the ground, then grab the tip of the tail and pick it up, leaving the viper hanging in the air. Its head can't get at the tip of its tail or the human hand holding it. Its field of action is so limited that if you hold it with your arm outstretched it can do you no harm. Its spell is broken. Massimo's father, who hated the vipers with the deepest loathing, wanted to see them suffer.

On the evening of a successful day spent hunting snakes there would be a corked two-litre bottle on the table at supper, with the viper dying slowly inside it. Massimo's father never took his eyes off the snake constantly trying to find a way up and out, slithering down the smooth glass wall, coiling together at the bottom only to try again, looking for a way of escape from the prison where it had less and less air in which to survive. It took many hours for the snake to perish, and Massimo's father watched its agonising death. He ate, drank and talked, bragging triumphantly, and felt proud. When he was drunk he would taunt the snake, urging it to be brave and tapping the bottle over and over again with a fork when the viper coiled up, ready to give in. And he cursed it, counting up all the sheep on the conscience of its kind, wishing them to all the devils in all the pits of hell.

Despite Massimo's mother's pleas for reason, his father insisted that the children should stay in the room and not go to bed until the snake had finally stopped twitching and died. Uncle Gusto, known as the mute American, would watch the viper's fight with death, fascinated, and went happily up to his room in the attic when it was over. Massimo, who had learned as a child to kill creatures, skin hares, shoot birds or put a sick dog out of its misery with a well-aimed bullet, hated those evenings when his father amused himself with the vipers.

Once, when Massimo was still little and both respected and feared the vipers, his mother put the bottle containing the snake to one side while she was clearing the table and his father was fetching wine from the shed. Someone knocked the bottle over, it fell to the floor, broke, and set the viper free. Massimo's mother and the children stood on the table trembling, and his father, who was obviously frightened too, left the house swearing volubly to fetch Don Aurelio's famous cat from Campanolo. People always sent for this cat when they had or suspected they had vipers in the house, the shed, the cellar or the stable. Don Aurelio, who had a car, came back with Massimo's father and the cat, transporting her in a cardboard carton from an orange firm. They took out the cat – a perfectly ordinary twelve-year-old tabby – shut her in the house, left a window open just a crack and waited. Neighbours came to join them, and soon half the village was standing outside the house. The women quietly cursed their menfolk who wouldn't listen to reason and were rash enough to keep bringing vipers indoors, the men swore at the women for their clumsiness. They laid bets on the cat and the viper, while Don Aurelio praised his cat (whose name was Binca) at length, as if he were preaching a sermon, not without emphasising how dangerous this whole venture was, and how easily it could mean the end for his unique pet, the best of all cats. Time went on, and Don Aurelio was telling them yet again how Binca first won fame. At six months old she was out with Don Aurelio in the garden, where he was digging over a bed and suddenly came upon a viper. He was about to hit it with his spade when he saw Binca and the snake looking at each other, squaring up for a fight. An exciting spectacle, and the Don wanted to watch it. What would the outcome be? His left arm raised and crooked at an angle, he demonstrated the snake and its field of action, using his right fist to mime the cat keeping at a safe distance. The viper, he continued, was a cowardly creature and tried to escape. When it thought the cat was no danger, because she stood there perfectly still, it turned away, and at that moment the clever cat jumped for its neck and bit it just behind the head, exactly where you have to catch a viper with the forked branch. Binca did that at only six months old! After this Don Aurelio, believing that he had recognised the cat's gifts, asked all the local farmers to bring him any live vipers they caught. He always put Binca in a room, placed the snake imprisoned in its bottle in front of her, then shot at the bottle through the window with an air gun and waited. And every time – sometimes quite quickly, sometimes after an hour or even two – she jumped out of the window victorious, the dead viper dangling from her mouth. In time he taught her to lay the snake at his feet when he whistled.

She's got twenty-four vipers to her credit.

Bloody hell!

Good for her!

What a cat!

Always a fight to the death.

One of them will be the end of her.

That's a fact.

You can't train a cat to do it.

No, they have to have talent.

She's got talent.
Her first viper at only six months!
Bloody hell!
Good for her!
One of them will be the end of her.
Yes, so it will.
She's getting on now.
One of them, maybe this one.
Yes, could be.
Then she'll be dead.
Won't be worth anything any more.
That's right.

Applause burst out. Binca, admired and applauded by one and all, came jumping out of the window with the viper dangling from her mouth, went over to the proud Don Aurelio and put the snake down in front of him. He stroked and praised the cat lavishly, then put her back in the orange carton, picked up the viper, announced that it had the honour of being her twenty-fifth, and then – as one returns someone a piece of property lent out only briefly – handed it back to Massimo's father. Massimo's father took it, his face suddenly twisted in a grimace, the veins on his temples swelled, he went red in the face, struck the snake on the ground again and again, holding it fast by the tail, threw it well away from him, followed it, trampled on it, shouted and roared until all the fury was out of his body. The onlookers were so horrified to hear him uttering such frightful oaths in front of Don Aurelio that later, while Massimo's mother was fetching payment in kind, in the form of cheese, eggs, ham and salami, the priest took the precaution of hearing his confession, not wishing to leave him in something so far from a state of grace.

It was the war did it to him, Massimo's mother always said, apologetically. Will the Lord forgive him? she timidly asked Don Aurelio, as he got back into his car, loaded down with gifts.

The Lord has forgiven him already.

Massimo, small as he still was then, could understand his father's outburst. That viper had preferred to fight the cat, had opted out of the agonising death intended for it, thus cheating his father out of his entire ritual of revenge. You could only guess how many of the blows and curses expended on the dead viper were really meant for Massimo's mother and her carelessness.

The real problem for his mother, the children, the rest of the family and the villagers was that his father wished the death suffered by the vipers on all his enemies, on thieves and murderers, people who watered wine, the police, politicians and Germans, pizza bakers and the civil servants in the land registry, the priest of San Nazzarro, the football team of Juventus Turin, the gravedigger in Ronco who refused to bury his brother who committed suicide, the doctor in Como who had operated on him for a war wound, his brother-in-law Silvio and the entire population of Ticino. He was not an easy man to live with, and Massimo's mother, although she knew better, always blamed it on the damn war. When his father died of a heart attack Massimo, who was about fourteen at the time, heard his mother telling her sister that it was an injustice crying out to heaven for a man who had wished the cruellest of deaths on so many to die such a merciful death himself, a death to be desired as a happy release.

Massimo sits down, collects water in the hollow of his hand, drinks, wipes the sweat from his brow. Down below him on the other and lower hill, directly above the village, lies another village, Oggia, which has been deserted for over thirty years now. Like the farm up here, it can be reached only along the mule paths. It was down these paths that the inhabitants of Oggia used to take milk and cheese to the village and then on to the lake, to Menaggio, Porlezza, Cadenabbia, to the big hotels or the little delicatessen stores, to private villas or on board ships.

Once upon a time, so the old folk say, before there were refrigerators, they used to hack blocks of ice from the mountain, pack them on the mules and take them down to the hotels.

There lies Oggia, sleeping in the sun. Little grey stone houses, crooked roofs made partly of stone and partly of wooden beams, held in place by chunks of rock fixed to wires. House beside house, huddling together, keeping each other cool or warm, inhabited now by rats, mice and dormice. Only the little church, not much bigger than the houses, modest and inconspicuous, stands a little way off on a hill. To Massimo, who was a child when the last inhabitants moved out, Oggia has always been a place of mystery, full of stories from another age. As boys he and his friends sometimes came up here to sit in the dimly lit, deserted cottages, smoking and playing gambling games, surrounded by the musty cloak of scary stories told by the old folk as they sat beside the fire in the evenings, murmuring, nodding, toothless, sparing of their words as they tried to remember names.

Valerio!

That was it, Valerio!

Valerio and Giambattista!

And the rope!

Ah yes, the rope!

In Antonio's bar up in Oggia.

Fernando, wasn't it?

No, Antonio was running the bar then.

Fernando's son.

Son-in-law.
That's it, son-in-law.
Valerio and Giambattista.
Brothers, they were.
It was because they were brothers.
And Teresa was dead by then.
That's right.
So there was only the two of them left.
Valerio and Giambattista.
The name wasn't Giambattista.
Yes, Giambattista, he was a blacksmith, worked in San Nazzarro.
Right, but his name wasn't Giambattista.
Yes, it was.
No.
What was it, then?
He was a blacksmith.
Worked in San Nazzarro.
With Roberto the fat blacksmith.
That's right.
Yes, that's right.
But his name was Gianluca.
That's it!
Gianluca.
That was his name, yes.
Yes.
Valerio's brother, he was.
Valerio who caught vipers with his bare hands.
That's right.
Always fighting, the pair of them.
Cursing and swearing.
It's a wonder they didn't knock each other's heads in.
You're right there.
That's how it was.

In Fernando's bar every day.
Antonio's.
In Antonio's bar.
Because Antonio was running the bar when it happened.
The pair of them, always in the bar.
And always drunk.
The two of them alone in that house, no women.
Never any women.
And no other pleasures in life.
Just Oggia and San Nazzarro and Oggia and the bar.
Antonio's bar.
Always quarrelling.
Valerio and Gianluca.
Shouting their heads off.
I'll kill you, I'll murder you, by the dog-god!
By the dog-god and every Sacred Host in these damn valleys, I'll murder you!
Like that, it was, every day.
Like that every evening.
Then staggering home to bed.
Same bed.
Both in one bed.
Always drunk, by the dog-god.
By the pig-god too.
Scandalous, all the Sacred Hosts in these valleys.
These damn valleys!
And then one evening.
Ah yes, that evening.
Valerio comes into the bar on his own.
Gianluca.
No, no, it was Valerio.
Gianluca was the elder.
That's right.
And Valerio was the younger.

And the younger brother was alone in the bar.
That evening.
Valerio.
That's right, him.
Saying nothing.
No shouting, no cursing.
So Antonio's worried.
Can't make it out.
What's up, Valerio?
He . . .
Where's Gianluca?
He . . .
He what?
Nothing, no answer.
So Antonio?
Asks more and more questions.
The others too.
My uncle Riccardo was there.
He lived in Oggia too.
And Silvio the wine merchant.
That's right, Ferruccio the wine merchant's father.
He was there.
Silvio.
So they're all asking questions.
What's up with Gianluca?
Why isn't Gianluca here?
And then?
Ah yes, then!
Oh, dear heaven!
By all the Sacred Hosts of the valleys, damn the lot of you!
Pig-gods and pig-gods again!
So what does Valerio say?
He says, just imagine, he says:
How could he be here when he's there?

Says Valerio.
Where?
In the stable.
In the stable?
'Sright, in the stable. Gianluca's in the stable.
So damn it all, what's Gianluca doing in the stable?
Why, says Valerio, what do you think he's doing?
Well, what?
What would he be doing? Hanging there, that's what.
Hanging there?
From the hook, that's right, from the hook.
From the hook?
Yes, from the hook where we pull the wether up to skin it, that hook.
Hanging there, you said?
And he laughs.
Not right in the head.
They'd got nothing in their brains.
Bicycles in their brains.
Both of them.
Right.
So everyone goes off to the stable.
And there he was, hanging.
Hanged himself, he had.
So Valerio goes on sitting in the bar, calm as you please.
Now do you see why he can't be here? Ha, ha, ha!
Not right in the head.
Neither of them.
And now one of them dead.
Hanged himself and nobody knows why.
The bicycle in his brain.
So they take Gianluca down.
Don't need to call any doctor.
Dead as a doornail, he is.

They take him down to the village on a mule.
To the doctor's house.
They put him on the table for the doctor to write out the death certificate.
And Valerio goes on sitting in the bar.
Laughing.
Calm as you please.
As if nothing had happened.
Drinking and laughing.
So then Antonio closes for the night.
And Valerio staggers home.
No Gianluca no more.
No cursing and swearing.
And no bloody carrying on about the Sacred Host.
No more shouting: I'll murder you.
Because one of them's dead already.
And one of them's nothing without the other, that's how come it turned out like it did.
They'd just got back up again with the mule.
So then they could take Valerio down from the hook too.
And put him on the mule.
And back they go to put him on the doctor's table.
For him to write out the death certificate.
In Padua where he studied, said the doctor, they preserved brains like those two had in spirits.
Spiritus Sanctus, said the priest, and they buried Gianluca and Valerio. Ever since then folk have called them the swearing brothers when they speak of them. They buried them under the gutter of the little church where suicides were put.

Massimo, Franco-Francone and Bruno sat there smoking their first cigarette, staring up at the hook with the old folk's stories in their ears.

They piss themselves when they do it.

Who do?

Suicides.

Who says?

My father.

They piss themselves when their necks break.

Says my father.

Some even get a hard-on.

Who says?

My brother.

Your brother ever hanged himself, has he?

Or had a hard-on?

It was the priest in Roncolo, the one that hanged himself back then.

Hanged himself. So he did.

And he had a hard-on.

Says my uncle.

For once in his life at least.

Says my uncle.

9

Once before, weeks before Alessandro suddenly turned up in the yard, he had been to the station here, he'd run away from her, he had stared up into the high dome, overwhelmed by this building and its huge dimensions that made a human being no more than an ant, and he was overwhelmed by the pain of parting too, haunted by thoughts of her there in that room where the sunlight never came, of lying beside her, of her smell, her words, her body that spoke to him of many other men, of her sudden passion and her sad indifference, her furious screaming and her defiant silence. He had called Bruno's mobile.

I'm coming home.

He said.

Good.

Said Bruno.

And then there was Renata suddenly, weeping, and they went back to her place, climbed the steep, dark, dirty stairs, his heart at odds with itself, and fell into her bed.

But this time the words Renata flung at him after Alessandro's appearance killed all lust, all desire. No, there was no going back for Massimo now. When he boarded this train to Como his thoughts had long since flown ahead of it, flying over the lake, up the mountains, stopping at the trees in the farmyard and the house, avoiding the view of the peak of the Madonnina, falling into Severina's outstretched arms.

He found a window seat, sat down, felt his heart beating faster when the train at last set off, making the idea of going back to the city more and more improbable, and finally impossible.

For the second time in Massimo's life he was travelling the Milan to Como stretch of the railway line. On the first occasion with her and her companions, that wild, crazy, inebriated bunch, he'd seen nothing, noticed nothing, he didn't look out of the train window once. He had paid no attention to what he saw now as the train passed the back yards of the city, the country, the world. As if the fine streets didn't exist, the handsome classy villas, the gardens with their palm trees, the palazzi or even the imposing station façade, no, the train moved straight from a siding to run along past the back yards. Past garages, workshops, coal merchants, small factories, haulage firms, scrapyards. There seemed to be nothing but industrial estates and grey suburbs behind the magnificent big city railway terminus stations. Children playing on dirty asphalt waved, women on balconies that were close enough to touch ignored the train, hung out their washing, fed canaries, called to the children down below. Again and again, in between the industrial complexes, warehouses and tanks, piles of rubble and garbage, stood long buildings with apartments stacked on top of one another, all just like each other, all the balconies the same, the same clothes from the same stores hanging out on them, the same TV programme switched on in the dark living-rooms beyond the balconies, advertising the products sold in the shops on the streets of this suburban area. Cars, noodles, furniture, coffee, ham, liqueurs. Massimo knew these shops. They faced the motorway, waving all kinds of seductive giant ads at travellers. Gleaming glass façades, gigantic furnishing stores, big office blocks, coffee-roasting establishments, garages, filling stations, supermarkets, and again furnishing stores, more and more of them. He had once seen them, years ago, when he went to watch the motor racing at Monza with friends. The shops facing the streets were like stage sets, like a child's puppet theatre, brightly painted in front, but behind the curtain there were just rough planks hammered together, and the rest of the buildings lay behind them, storehouses, toilets, courtyards and back yards, garbage tips. It was through these scenes the train was passing.

More grey apartment blocks, then dreary little gardens, rabbit hutches, water butts, compost heaps. And rubbish everywhere – the rubbish of decades thrown out of train windows. Then, at last, trees and bushes, finally a graveyard with a climbing plant growing over its wall into the brightly coloured cars of a scrapyard the other side, through the broken windows, over the roofs, as if intent on giving Nature back what had been taken from her. It would make its way on into the city, covering and growing over everything that Massimo had just passed, clambering over the roofs of the buildings and garages and storehouses, over the fences, along the walls, at some point reaching the great station and putting it out of action. It would grow through the railway tracks and the kiosks, the trains and the booking windows, it would wind its way round people and strangle them, and eat its way on into the city.

Massimo woke up. He had been asleep. How long? Not very long. Or had he? There were meadows outside now, gardens, little farms, goats, a few sheep, chickens, cats, a barking dog, people working in the warm sun, a different sky, mountains, the gleaming lake, ancient ochre-yellow houses, cypresses, oleanders, Como.

The station. The train stopped, Massimo got out. There was the familiar old blue bus outside on the forecourt, the bus that drove along the lake and back three times a day. The bus that picked up people from the mountains and took them back again, farmers needing a new suit, or wanting the notary to draw up documents for the sale of a few square metres of land to a neighbour, others on business with authorities of some kind, women dolling themselves up for a shopping trip round the boutiques, usually in couples, excitement and expectation in their faces in the morning, tired now that their errands were done, secondary-school pupils, a few giggling adolescent girls who worked as chambermaids in the lakeside hotels and were full of gossip, housewives, commuters glad to have a job here, maybe as a cleaner, so they didn't have to work for those stuck-up Swiss in nearby Lugano. They were all in the bus now. Mario had been driving it for so many years that he knew almost everyone who got in.

Hi, Luca, been on the booze again?

Hi, Mario, yup, been on the booze.

Why now, Vittorina, what pretty things have we been buying, then? Underclothes, is it, lovely underwear, oh, won't your husband just –

Shut up, do, Mario!

Aha, here's our Signora Travella! Oh, signora, by all the saints, do give me your hairdresser's number, I wouldn't mind looking twenty years younger myself!

Oh, Mario, you and your compliments!

You're welcome, signora, ah, if it was always so easy! Why, who's this, then?

Hi, Mario!

Hi, Massimo!

Back here in town, are you?

Yes.

Long time no see.

Yes, it's a long time since I was here.

So you're back in town again today?

Yes, back today.

Well then – ah, here comes Luigi! Always at the last minute.

Yes, only just made it. Hi, Mario.

Hi, Luigi!

Why, if that isn't Massimo! I don't believe it! Where did you spring from?

Oh, just dropped from heaven.

Dropped from heaven, eh? Flew here, did you? Simply flew here from Germany, is that right?

What do you mean, Germany?

Weren't you in Germany?

Me in Germany?

You weren't?

What would I be doing in Germany?

Yes, what would you be doing there?

Well, go on, what would I be doing there?

Whatever you've been doing wherever you were.

Ah, wherever I was. So where was that, Luigi?

With that woman, know what I mean?

That's right, Luigi.

Ha, ha, ha.

Ha, ha, ha.

You're a devil of a fellow, eh?

Ha, ha, ha.

I'll say!

And how are you, Luigi?

How was Luigi? He didn't say, which was unusual, because he usually came straight out with everything that happened to him and anything that came into his mind. Luigi said nothing. The mere question had struck him dumb, and he still said nothing as the bus made its way along the winding lakeside road, hooting loudly, barging its way through, brushing past the walls of houses standing close together on both sides of the road with a millimetre to spare, driven with great determination by Mario in line with his timetable. People got out, got in, made their way down the bus, stowed luggage, found a seat, chattered, greeted one another or said goodbye. Some of them knew Massimo. They nodded: Hi, back in town again? Yes, have to go to town now and then. But what on earth was the matter with Luigi? Usually you had to avoid Luigi if you wanted to be left in peace or look through the sports paper, because Luigi kept inexorably, inescapably talking away at you. Now Luigi sat there saying nothing, silenced by the mere inquiry after his welfare. He stared at the lake, made chewing motions with his few remaining teeth, and sweated.

Hell, Luigi, what's wrong?

Luisa.

He said it mysteriously, with a dismissive wave of his hand.

What's the matter with Luisa?

That's what I'd like to know too, what's the matter with Luisa?

Is she sick?

Sick? Yes, sick. Sick in the head.

Sick, thought Massimo, sick, no, she's crazy. But she always was crazy. So was Luigi. Didn't we always say: What a bit of luck, two crazy people getting together? Luigi and Luisa, who built a tree-house while they were engaged and spent their wedding night up in the tree. There was even a picture of it in the paper. The two of them loved each other, and lived with their craziness, their muddled heads, the peculiar ideas they so often shared, as if they had sprung from a single head and a single mind. They always provided the village with something to talk about, something for people to laugh at, grin over as they tapped their foreheads. And the secret was that each thought the other perfectly normal. Although they considered the people around them, the other villagers, their neighbours, a little crazy. Yes, Luigi and Luisa often couldn't help laughing at them, but they got on with them all right.

She's sick, then, is she?

Sick in the head, very, very sick in the head.

Massimo looked at the lake where the *Arrow of the Valleys*, a fast hovercraft, was skimming the waves like a bird, just above the water, as if driven by the breaking crests. Up in front Mario was shouting like a fairground barker at a Dutchman in a caravan, who was making his way at snail's pace through the narrow streets.

Get a move on, can't you? You and your goddam living-room on wheels! Move yourself! Look at that, will you, what a nerd! Got all their household goods with them, by the pig-god, dammit, but can't drive! Won a driving licence in the lottery! Living-room, bedroom, kitchen, the lot! Bringing the whole shooting match along! Bloody Dutch! I can't wait to see them stopping for a picnic bang in the middle of the street! To hell with the Dutch, every last one of them!

Luigi, who had usually been of the opinion that every moment in which you said nothing was time stolen from the Lord God, stared dully ahead. He seemed to be hearing nothing, taking nothing in. What could all this about Luisa be? For the first time ever, Massimo dared not ask Luigi a question, because he was afraid of hearing that Luisa really had gone mad, so mad that even crazy Luigi himself sat there like a sad but normal man, telling no stories of other people who, in his opinion, were crazy.

There had been fears for Luisa before, ten or twelve years ago, when the boy had his accident. Luisa and Luigi had gone years without having children. She suffered two miscarriages, and there was a baby who died a few days after birth, just like little Sebastiano, indeed in the same year.

Luisa and Severina both suffered a great deal, each in her own way. You didn't see Severina's grief outwardly, but at home the child was still alive for her. For weeks she laid a place at table for an imaginary person, the cradle still stood in the bedroom for months, and all winter she went to the grave daily, stood or sat or knelt there for hours, freezing, praying or blaming the Lord, no one knew which, because it was all done in silence. Luisa, on the other hand, lamented her sorrows out loud. She bought things for the child in second-hand shops and in town, baby food, toys, clothes. She talked about the progress he was making, and how like Luigi he was, for the child was a boy. All day she talked to the baby without a break, and by night she called his name out of the window again and again, in desperate fits of shouting. People closed their windows or turned up the volume of their TVs so as not to have to hear her. The men playing bowls outside the bar shook their heads, went into the bar and bought a grappa for Luigi, poor devil, Luigi who couldn't understand what was going on and what had happened to his Luisa. There was nothing they could say, however. In the face of grief they were all usually mute.

Valerio! Valerio! she shouted, as if he could come down to her in angelic form.

Unlike Severina, Luisa was soon pregnant again and had a healthy son, whom they once more called Valerio. It seemed like a miracle that he grew into a bright, intelligent, good-looking boy, when so many children of really clever or just normal people went bad and caused all kinds of anxiety.

Luisa idolised her son, and Severina, so Massimo sensed, was jealous, for she saw it as an injustice of fate. She herself did not become pregnant again. He was always going on at Severina, quarrelling with her, shouting angrily at her, because he wanted them both to go to the doctor to be examined, but she wouldn't hear of it.

Once Massimo did ask the doctor, down at the bar, what was the matter with his wife.

She doesn't have a baby because she doesn't want one.

Oh no, doctor, she did want a baby, she'd love to be a mother, she's suffering terribly.

All the same, she's resisting it. She doesn't want to replace her dead Sebastiano with someone else. He lives on in her and for her.

That's not easy to understand, doctor.

The way women think and feel often isn't easy to understand, Massimo.

You're right, doctor.

They don't think and feel the same way we do.

Well, they have to have the children.

Exactly, Massimo, that's it.

And then the accident happened. The boys and their silly bet, Valerio, the hero who now held a sad record, racing down the mountain on his motorbike, breaking his neck on the rocks before his mother's eyes.

For a whole year she called that name into the night again. Valerio! Valerio!

Then she went back to her normal craziness, her life with Luigi. She scarcely went to the graveyard any more. Severina sometimes put a flower on the grave of the two Valerios when she went to visit Sebastiano.

So what had happened now?

Something must have happened.

How do you mean, sick in the head, Luigi? Come on, tell me what's wrong. Haven't lost your tongue, have you, old friend?

Luigi was breathing heavily, panting and perspiring, laboriously seeking words, stringing them together into half-sentences, stammering, stuttering, spitting the words out like a series of curses.

The weather, see, the weather. The weather in March, you know. Hear about it where you were, did you? The weather, all that rain, rained for weeks, bucketing down from the sky. And the mountains coming down and the rock slides, all in the streets, chaos in the streets and everywhere, dammit, chaos, by all the saints, haven't seen weather like that in a long time. Not for ten or twenty years, they said on TV. No weather like it in years, they said, I mean such rain, and the water washing everything down, mountains coming downhill all over the place. So it was on the Thursday, I couldn't go to work. The bus couldn't go, nothing. So I'm sitting in the bar, drinking with Franco-Francone and Bruno, and yes, Ferruccio was there, we were in Teresa's bar that afternoon. At three o'clock. So Albino comes in shouting: The graveyard! The graveyard! Just stands there shouting, see? The graveyard! Just that: The graveyard!

He had shouted it out himself, as Albino must have done. The passengers in the bus looked at them. Some of them were smiling. They knew Luigi. Crazy Luigi has finally gone right off his head again, they thought, rather pleased. He's been so quiet recently. It almost made a person begin to wonder about his state of health or anyway his state of mind. But now he seemed to be the old Luigi again, crazy Luigi. So that was all right.

What about the graveyard?

It had come down, right down into the street. Washed down, the churchyard wall broke and came down, the whole first row of graves right there outside the barber's door, down in the street, right into the square, see? Our own grave and ten others, all down in the street. And the bones and the skulls, and the whole village was there, the women, the children who weren't at school, and all the wreaths off old

Alborghetti's freshly dug grave and his coffin caught in the bushes, half-way down the slope, hanging in the air. Could come right down any moment. And suddenly there's Luisa beside me.

Valerio! she screams. Valerio!

The bus entered a tunnel, and under cover of the darkness Luigi told him out loud what had caused the sickness in Luisa's head.

There he is, our boy Valerio, lying in the dirt, the skeleton, the whole skeleton and the yellow jacket! That yellow jacket, good as new, it was plastic, see? The yellow jacket we buried him in, and the skeleton inside it. Poor Luisa!

Poor Luisa, yes. Oh, good God!

She couldn't bear it, Massimo. It was more than she could bear, it was just too much for her.

Jesus and Mary, yes.

Luigi had slouched forward, burying his face in his hands, and was weeping. Massimo sat beside him feeling helpless, put his arm around the man, who was trembling all over, and looked out of the bus window. There was the hovercraft on the lake again. In the end, thought Massimo, what with the time it takes to moor it, it's no faster than the bus.

Why did we do it, Massimo, why did we bury him in that jacket?

Because you meant well.

He was so proud of it, you see.

I know, Luigi, I know.

10

Severina is coming downhill to the house. There sits the old woman on the wooden bench, you can scarcely make her out, she has almost merged with the weathered, seasoned wood. Her eyes immediately fasten on Severina's figure, following it, not letting it go, registering and silently commenting on her haste, her rapid, hunted look, the way she stumbles and throws down the half-full pannier. As usual, the old woman follows Severina's actions with a pair of eagle eyes and mild derision. What's the matter now, she wonders, is someone coming? Franco-Francone, maybe? Is that any reason to run home in such agitation, stumbling, in such a hurry? Or is it her father Alessandro, coming to shout at her again and try to make her talk? There must be something, she must have taken something into her head again, because after all she's crazy, as crazy as Luisa down there.

The old woman, Severina thinks, doesn't know anything yet of what she's been waiting for all year, what has dominated all her thoughts and feelings. She's not about to give her the satisfaction, she won't tell her anything, above all she doesn't want to witness her joy, her triumph over herself, Severina. Severina wishes the old woman dead, simply dead. Don't people die of a joyful surprise, a merciful death, when the heart that was beating only for this moment suddenly stands still, as if it has done its work? This is the death she wishes for the old woman. If there's such a thing as dying of joy, then in God's name let her die. She must not witness his return to his wife. Mustn't triumph over her, mustn't be able to look at her any more, always questioning: Yes, so now what's wrong with you, here he is, my dear son, your husband, go on, start talking, speak, forgive him if there's anything to forgive. Everything she said in the afternoons and on the long evenings of the cold weather that forced them into almost physical proximity by the fire to keep warm, all her words, all her remarks, all her glances, let them stay where they are in her. Let her not be able to say any of it any more. Let her be the mute one, let her be silenced. Dear Lord, give me a miracle and I'll give you one back, the one and only miracle I have. The miracle that has made me able to survive and must be my weapon now, my shield, my defence, my pride. And my love too. Dear Lord God, silence her for ever now, in this hour, and I'll speak again at once.

Yes, well, the Lord! The Lord God! How she has prayed to him, how she has called on him, laid her wishes at his feet, begging, oh, bring him back to me, bring the man back, make it not have happened. I need that man, I do love him, I want to be with him always, bring him back to me, dear Lord!

The Lord.

Did the Lord ever listen to her?

No.

And where was he when little Sebastiano died at scarcely three days old, unbaptised, innocent? What has he ever done for her, how has he rewarded her faithfulness to him, the faithfulness she showed even after Sebastiano's death, reciting rosaries and Our Fathers out of a full heart and true soul down by the grave? Or is Massimo's return the reward? Is that your reward, O Lord, is that your will? It is his will, it must be! Yes, it had been a sign after all!

She has so often cut wood on the hills, shorn the sheep, mowed grass for the rabbits, deep in her work, and suddenly heard the humming tone of the cable when someone struck it to announce his arrival. But what about this time? She had put the sickle down, shielded her eyes with her hand, looked to the end of the path and saw him, a small dot. Was that it? Yes, she is sure that was it. Wasn't the Lord God telling her: Severina, here comes your husband, I have sent him back to you, look, do you see? And it is God's great power when, on a starlit night, you look up to the heights of the sky and see a shooting star, racing down to the horizon fast as lightning and sinking below it. You wouldn't see it unless the Lord told you: Look, and then it happens in that split second. And now it has pleased the Lord to send her husband back to her. Why? What is the Lord's will?

Didn't he also command Massimo to go and leave her? Or does the Lord have no power over him? Could there be quite different forces at work in a man, telling him to do whatever he has taken into his head? Do men act against God's will? Can they do that and go unpunished by the Lord? She was once going to ask Don Roberto this question, but when she faced him she didn't dare, for she suddenly realised: Don Roberto is only a man too. How would he know, any more than any other man? No, men act against God's will, because it's men who go away, leave wives and children, stand at the back of the church at Mass, pray without much devotion and leave divine service before the priest has said Amen. They do it because there's a godless power in them. So why doesn't God punish men for breaking his commandments, particularly the sacrament of marriage? Why? Is it because he's only a man too? Is God really a man?

Severina takes the sickle to the shed, passes the bird-cage, sees the last pathetic inmates still inside it, those that didn't freeze in winter or die of loneliness or their struggles with the wire netting. She opens the door, shoos the birds out with her hands, making them flutter up in alarm. None of them leave their prison. They are confused. Severina hits the wire netting with the palms of her hands, the birds flutter round in surprise, find the way out at last, but they don't know what to make of their sudden freedom. Some just sit helplessly on the ground, others fly a little way off into a bush or a tree. They'll want to soar into the air, looking longingly for their companions, and they'll realise that they can't fly, their wings have been clipped. Severina goes hastily into the house, all in a rush, goes to the bedroom, snatches up a blanket, takes down the wedding photo from the wall, stares briefly at the crucifix above the bed, and leaves the room. She takes refuge in the loft. And the old woman sits outside, thinking how she once sat here as a child, trying in vain to work out how many years ago that is, looking up at the trees as if they could answer her. She drops off to sleep, never guessing that in a few moments her old heart will almost stop for joy and fulfilment.

II

The old woman had been sitting like that last year too: upright, almost motionless, staring at the path along which her son had gone with the intoxicated strangers, had disappeared, not to come back next morning or the morning after either. She sat there for two days and two nights, the image of reproach, her defiant face saying: You drove him away, it serves you right, you drove him away, he had to go because you were a bad wife to him. At first her reproaches showed only in her face, but when she gave up her look-out post and went back to the bench by the fireside they became the material of long, mournful lamentations and sly digs, lying over the long evenings like acrid smoke. She put roots of ill-will down in the house, and they clung on. Her tirades of hatred for Severina even upset the animals in the stable. She turned night into day, she never rested, she went on and on even when her daughter-in-law, shaken by convulsive weeping, was sobbing with her hands over her ears. Severina didn't want to hear it any more, always the same as it was. She felt desperate. She ran out of doors, calling his name out into the night, down into the valley, up to the mountain, to the peak of the Madonnina. The silence that followed derided her.

Severina had taken refuge from the old woman in the loft, that low-ceilinged little space above the kitchen-cum-living-room. This was where she slept. This was where she lay awake, listened to the night noises, the creaking of the trees, the hooting of the owls, the faint scurrying of dormice in the shed, the fluttering of the bats. And she felt as if she could hear the mocking laughter of the men in the bar down in the village.

And in the morning there sat the old woman again, a whole lifetime lived almost to the end written on her face, with nothing left but the hope of seeing her dear son again, the hope that would keep her alive now. She would freeze her features in that expression. How long, Severina wondered, how long would she hold out? Would he ever come back? Would she ever hear him striking the cable? Would he stay with the strange woman now? What was it about that strange woman, Severina asked herself, what did she mean? She tried to picture the woman, and found that she hardly could. In her panic at Massimo's state of confusion she had seen only him, not the woman whose face she could no longer picture. How could that be? Doesn't a jealous woman notice every feature, every wrinkle, every gesture, every word and the sound of it? Don't you keep recalling them so that you can hate and despise them? Severina couldn't hate the woman because she meant nothing to her. Men leave, say women with experience of such things, men leave because they want to leave. There comes a certain moment of time when they just want to leave, it's not because some particular person has come into their lives. So it has nothing to do with that woman. It could have been anyone.

But if that's really true, thought Severina, why did he want to leave now? They hadn't quarrelled. Everything was all right. They had settled down to their life with its tasks and its duties. She had even accepted the old woman for his sake. After all, the old woman was his mother. She allowed him his adventures down in the bar in the evening, and then in Rosanna's bed. She had never asked questions, never even showed that she knew about it. And she had even come to terms with not having any more children after little Sebastiano's death. They didn't talk about it any more, they didn't mention it. It was all so long ago. Sebastiano would be a grown man now, he'd have a car and a girlfriend, he might be a lorry driver travelling all over Europe, sending picture postcards home from everywhere. Or perhaps he'd be a carabiniere down in the police station in a fine uniform, a man of importance, respected by all and slightly feared by some. Whatever he might have been today, he wouldn't be the little Sebastiano he still was to her. Her innocent little Sebastiano.

Now Massimo had left. But typically for him, he hadn't done it secretly, quietly, on the sly. He had left before all eyes, the way he once soared over the valley on the cableway with the dog, to general admiration and applause. He had gone out of Severina's life the way he came into it: smiling, proud, upright, crazy. Is he crazy, maybe? Did he do it to make them all admire him again down in the village? Will they really admire him, thereby pouring scorn on her? They'll envy him, the men who just dream of such adventures on sultry evenings in the bar, or at most talk about them longingly, only to stagger back to the familiarity of home. Will any of them think of her, and her grief and despair? Franco-Francone might.

Good old Franco-Francone.

Poor Severina, he'll say to his wife. It was bound to happen, she'll say. He won't understand that, but he won't contradict her.

I mean, she'll say, when she couldn't have children and all. It's a wonder he stayed so long. Yes, well, someone else has come along now, a city girl, someone special. Did you see her?

Yes. In the bar.

So?

So what?

So what's she like?

Don't know. I only saw her.

Oh, listen to the man, will you! Don't know, I only saw her!

Well, so I did.

I mean is she pretty, is she young, is she fat, is she thin? Didn't you notice anything about her?

Skinny.

What else?

How do you mean, what else?

What does she do, does she have money, why has she taken Massimo off with her? That's what else.

He went with her.

Why?

He always wanted to find out something new.

It's because of her, that's why, it's because of Severina.

That's how they'll talk, thought Severina. She'll be inquisitive like all the women, he's a loyal friend to Massimo, so he can't say anything bad about him. They'll sit down to a good meal of pork, and while they eat it maybe they'll wonder who was to blame for Massimo and Severina not having any more children, and they'll think themselves lucky to have two daughters of their own who take after them in every way, weight included.

And the other women, thought Severina, they'll be eager to take their laundry out to the wash-house in the square, as if they didn't have washing machines at home. They'll put their heads together, gleeful, malicious, giggling, laughing at her scornfully, pretending to feel sorry for her, knowing better. Do you know about it, have you seen her? Yes, just imagine, hard to believe it, but the fact is it serves her right. She thought she could hang on to him all their lives. Well, if not one of us then why not a strange woman? They say he's madly in love with her, that's what I heard. We ought to ask Teresa, she knows everything. They say it was a positive orgy they had. An orgy, just think! My goodness, what will Rosanna say about that? Will she be upset? That's how they'll talk, and every one of them will feel better for it. They'll take their laundry home still dry to put it in the machine, and for now their own problems will seem small and insignificant.

But had he really gone away at all? Perhaps he was just down in the village repairing the fence, or perhaps someone had asked him to lend a hand with a major job of work, maybe he was helping Ferruccio to weld a garden gate, or driving wood down to the pizzeria beside the lake with Bruno. Maybe he'd let the strange woman go away. Feeling just a little bit ashamed of himself, he'd wait for a couple of days to go by and then come back up here as if nothing had happened. That's how it will be, thought Severina, I've let the old woman's lamentations send me crazy.

It was the third day. The old woman was hoarse with wailing out her complaints. She was weak and exhausted, and she fell silent. Severina cleaned the house, the stable and the shed, swept the yard, tidied up as if she had to get everything in perfect order for his return. And she decided firmly, over and over again, not to go looking for him, not to go down the mountain and ask questions, not to call his name out all round the village, because they would smile at her and deride her.

On the fourth day she did go looking for him, she went down and asked questions, and called his name out all round the village. And they smiled at her and derided her.

She felt it, she heard and sensed and saw it, it was the echo to her cries.

What do you mean, Severina? He's gone.

And who knows what will come of it.
No use shedding tears over a man.
Did you think he was faithful to you?
Him of all people!
Folk like that, they're always cheating on you.
The eagle's flown, has he?
He'll be back.
No one will keep him for long.
I'd be glad if my husband would go.
Me too.
It's the bad ones who stick around.
Like I always say, mine's good enough for me, he doesn't beat me.
A bird in the hand and all that.
Didn't you give him a good time, Severina?
Massimo of all people!
Always on the go.
You want to keep a better eye on a man like that.
Ask Teresa, she knows.
Or Rosanna.
Yes, ask Rosanna.
She's in mourning for him too.
But not running round the place calling his name.
That would be worth hearing!
Two of you running round the village calling for Massimo.
That would be worth hearing, like I say!
Men like him, they leave plenty of widows.
That was how they talked.
Severina didn't listen to it.
Yet she heard it. It drifted out of windows, echoed back from the walls, was there to be seen in their faces, the heads quickly disappearing behind net curtains spoke of it, the men looking down at the ground, with important business to do in a great hurry, gave it away. They knew everything, they

felt or pretended to feel sympathy, and suddenly, in defiance of all custom, minded their own business. Teresa spoke with relish of the bottles of grappa and champagne that had been taken into the house, and she mentioned the word orgy several times. Oh yes, they'd had an orgy, it went on into the small hours, until they all went off together in the bus, Rosanna could confirm everything, very likely she knew more.

Into the small hours!

An orgy!

Rosanna could indeed confirm it. She hadn't been able to close an eye all night, she said, and that was a fact. She'd felt ashamed of him, that's what, ashamed. She still felt ashamed, too. Just you go into the house, and you'll see what they got up to for yourself. Go on in, then. Severina did not go in. She left Rosanna to her own feelings, to the mixture of triumph, jealousy and grief which was overwhelming her, and Severina herself hurried back up the mountain. The scorn and derision rang in her ears for a long time, and she expected to see the same thing in the old woman's face up on the farm. Rosanna sought refuge and advice in her bottles of brightly coloured liqueurs.

Severina kept her own counsel for three more days. She worked hard enough for two, doing his work as well as her own, she chopped wood, finished repairing the stable roof, fed and mucked out the livestock, wrung a chicken's neck with grim fury, cooked for herself and the old woman, none of whose questions she answered. She said less and less. By night, weary as she was after all her work, she lay awake, hating the old woman's self-righteous snoring in the next room, listening to the noises outside, and on the third night she got out of bed, dressed, and went back down into the village under cover of dark. She walked fast, she knew the way, she went faster than usual on the way down, stumbling over stones and roots, falling over once, scrambling up, going on, in some strange kind of haste. Like an animal driven out of cover by the beaters. She crossed herself when she came to the crucifix in memory of Valerio who died in the accident.

When she went in search of Massimo she had not gone into the house. She had only called his name. She had no proof of what Rosanna and Teresa said; she hadn't wanted to see the humiliating evidence of his adventure, his conquest. What would she have seen? Just a rumpled bed, empty bottles, overfilled ashtrays. Now, unseen by Rosanna, as she thought, secretly, like a thief, she went into the house. It didn't smell stale and musty as usual when you came down from the mountain after several days, it smelled different, as it had never smelled before, a smell unfamiliar to Severina, one that constricted her throat and made her heart beat fast. She found the rumpled bed, the empty bottles, the overfilled ashtrays, and she realised that Rosanna and Teresa were right. There had been an orgy in here. Depressed, she went round the house. She was ashamed of him. Could that be true? Yes, she was ashamed of Massimo. Fury arose in her. She threw the bottles at the wall, tore the bedclothes off the bed, dragged them downstairs and burned them in the fireplace. Smoke billowed out at her, bringing tears to her eyes. She was wild with rage. But she stopped short when she saw the wedding picture on the mantelpiece. How proud she had been of it!

A handsome couple. Massimo, a head taller than Severina, looked protectively down at her, beaming; she was smiling rather hesitantly, seeking his protection. She had been in love at the time. She couldn't say, like the other women, that she had married for sensible reasons. She hadn't wanted anyone else. She had not so much as looked at or thought about anyone else. She had walked proudly through the village, she was happy when he kissed her in front of everyone, when she came in the evening to watch the game of bowls, where he would be holding forth. My little one, my treasure, my star, my dove, my little bird, such were the things he said to her, and she enjoyed it. How frightened she was, what a wallflower she had felt beside her beautiful sister, who had all the men looking at her. And she was well aware that behind her back many people wondered why Massimo hadn't chosen Anna.

Severina ran her fingers over the glass. The picture beneath the dust came clearer. For a moment it seemed as if looking at the picture might calm her down, but then the front door of the house opened, someone came down the passage to the kitchen, and in the reflection of the photograph frame Severina saw that Rosanna was standing in the doorway, silent and inquiring. The picture fell to the floor, and Severina stamped on it with unbridled fury until the glass was broken into a thousand fragments. Rosanna was still standing there in silence, as if she had some right here, as if she must administer punishment and discipline like a mother, as if she had to check up on something, as if Severina had asked her for help.

You must get people looking for him, Severina. You must report him missing.

What business is that of yours?

Cried Severina.

Weeping, Rosanna sat down on the steps outside the door of the house and buried her face in her hands.

I miss him too.

The young carabinieri who have just finished training always get given the table at the side of the room. Instead of seeing who's coming in at the main entrance or who's strolling along beside the lake, what you have here is a view of the river, not much of a river, a little brook really, where it flows sluggishly under a small bridge and out into the lake in a delta about twenty metres wide. Up in the mountains it is a torrential stream cascading down through deep ravines, but on the plain it loses its force and significance, and just trickles into the lake in thin rivulets. It brings with it everything thrown into the water higher up and now carried down to where notices proclaim, for people's information, 'No Garbage, Protect the Environment'. The river carries down plastic bags, rats, styrofoam cups, dead cats.

Adriano had been sitting here for some time now, looking out pensively for hours on end at this anteroom to his career, and dreaming. While he might not yet have any authority in the police station, none the less he was lord of this unofficial tip outside the window. Nothing there escaped his watchful eye. Six months ago he had found and brought in that miscarriage wrapped in a towel, which had been a great sensation, although its origin was never cleared up. And once, as he was sitting there dreamily, he suddenly saw a plastic bag in the shallows. It was moving more vigorously than could be accounted for by the water. He went out and found five live kittens. They ran about in the garden behind the police station, Adriano and the others fed them with scraps of the sandwiches they brought to work and played with them in off-duty breaks, until the police chief said: Those cats must go. Since the men were to have shooting practice the matter was easily settled, five service pistols firing six shots each, and the dead cats were thrown into the lake, where they would have ended up alive, but for the alert eye of Adriano the carabiniere.

In his day-dreams Adriano featured as a much-admired man, a successful man with money. He drove the Ferrari in Schumacher's place, he rode the racing bike instead of Pantani, he sang on stage, he acted in films, he was a Mafia boss who showed his enemies mercy, he walked arm in arm with the loveliest women, he graciously accepted the plaudits of the crowd, bathed in its admiration, travelled the world surrounded by beauty and wealth, luxury and acclamation. And of course he day-dreamed of the ideal woman, dreams of an extremely unrealistic nature by comparison with everything else he dreamt of, since for one thing the only woman he really knew was fat little Berta from the village, who had once let him touch her breasts, and for another he fancied any blonde whose bust size was slightly larger than Berta's. He lacked the experience to draw comparisons. He might want to be Schumacher in the Ferrari on a hundred days, but on every one of those days he fancied a different woman. In more unassuming moments he was the kindly, understanding police chief of all the carabinieri in the country, a man who had made it his business to open up glittering careers to junior carabinieri who sat at side tables with a view of unofficial rubbish tips, careers in which they could really prove their worth.

He couldn't dream at home. His mother wouldn't let him. She had made it clear at an early stage that God decides what career one does and does not follow, and there's no sense at all in dreaming of anything else.

Your father was a baker, you're a carabiniere, and Adriano Celentano is a famous man. And he's no cleverer than you and your father. But the Lord God has decided that Adriano Rossi senior will be a baker, Adriano Rossi junior will be a carabiniere, and Adriano Celentano will be a famous man. That's the will of the Lord. He puts people in the station of life where he needs them. So you don't want to dream, you should be content with your lot. The Lord needs carabinieri to keep order, and he's chosen you, even though you're not as bright as you might be! That was the way she went on.

Granny says I get the way I think from my father.

Don't you speak ill of your father, God rest his soul! Your father Adriano Rossi senior was the best baker in these valleys! And why was he so good? Because he baked the best bread. And why was his the best bread? Because he spat once into every loaf and crossed himself, a hundred times a day. And if he hadn't died of the smoking and his lungs and his tuberculosis and all that coughing he'd still be baking the best bread today! I'd like a little respect for your father, so you remember that, don't let it in one ear and out the other. Yes, and speaking of ears, you get yours from him too. You can go and visit his grave, weed it, put a few flowers on it and thank your father for giving you his ears! Being a baker he didn't need ears like that, but they're a real blessing for a carabiniere. And the good Lord will have had that in mind when he made you a carabiniere, because at least they keep your outsize service cap from falling over your face, like the caps of those idiot colleagues of yours. Off you go now and kill me a chicken. With the axe, not with that shotgun again! What's it doing here in the house anyway? Is that allowed? And when you've killed the chicken you can feed the pig and the rabbits. And don't go fighting with the neighbours' lads again or soon you won't have a tooth in your head, and we don't have money for the dentist. And keep your hands off that Berta! She's not fit for you! My son's too good for a girl who'll run after anyone with a prick between his legs, let me tell you. Oh, you men, we ought to take you by your pricks and shake you until you see reason! Don't you go off chasing the women like your father! And no dreaming! That brings nothing in! No drinking either! Drinking comes first and then dreaming. Drinkers and dreamers all land in the gutter.

That was life at home. She talked and worked all day long, and always sank into a heavy, dreamless sleep. Beneath her watchful gaze, which was everywhere, you always had to be doing something. She couldn't bear to see anyone just sitting about reading, watching TV or listening to music.

It's a waste of the good Lord's time, and his time isn't to be wasted.

She said.

So it was no wonder that unlike all others who are not carabinieri, Adriano was glad to go to work. Here in the guardroom, a handsome, high-ceilinged place, pleasantly cool even on hot summer days, there was peace and calm, because the natural apathy of his four colleagues meant that they spoke only when necessary. They sat under the picture of whoever was President of the Republic, working on papers when something could no longer be postponed, making it clear to anyone who came in wanting help that in most cases they themselves were helpless, since important affairs were decided higher up, not here, and they took it easy, in the certain knowledge that after work there was a mother, a wife or both waiting and insisting on having a thousand little jobs done. Because word had got around that the carabinieri could take it easy on duty.

Adriano had realised quite early on that enthusiasm was regarded as uncomradely. So here at the side table, in view of the little brook that began life as a modest spring high up in the mountains and finally became a lake, he dreamed his high-flown dreams. If anyone had seen his face through the window, the mouth slightly open with spittle at the corners, the two missing teeth and the half-closed eyes, he would have abandoned any idea of seeking advice, action and assistance in this place. One advantage of sitting at the side table was that Adriano was seldom obliged to figure as the guardian of law and order to any member of the public seeking advice. That summer afternoon last year, however, it did happen.

Looking through the window, he saw the woman coming over the bridge. He knew her: she was Severina, the wife of that man Massimo who had once flown over the valley with a load of timber. She was in a hurry, she looked energetic, she disappeared round the corner and soon afterwards entered the police station. What was she after here?

Adriano's colleagues Giuseppe, Nando and Rinaldo were out. Some woman from Naggio had called to say her husband had beaten her black and blue, only the police could help her. So the three had driven off to find out the man's reasons for beating his wife. And Gildo, fat Gildo, the eldest of them all, had gone out into the garden for a well-earned nap. Adriano therefore had to bestir himself.

What is it?

Oh, so it's you, Adriano the baker's son.

What is it?

Isn't your name Adriano too?

How can I help you, signora?

My husband Massimo is missing.

Name!

Massimo, I told you, you know him.

Your name, signora?

Oh, really! I'm Severina, for God's sake, you know me, Massimo's wife.

Can you prove it, signora?

Why would I have to prove it when you know me?

I'm not supposed to know you.

Your father was my father's sister-in-law's nephew. We're related, and you claim not to know me!

Everyone's equal before the law, and since I can't know everyone I'm not supposed to know anyone.

Nonsense!

It's the law.

It's nonsense!

And we keep the law in here, see?

Good God above!

I mean, the President himself could come in and I wouldn't be supposed to know him.

Do the police really put up with such idiocy?

The President would have to prove who he was.

Are you the only officer here?

All the others are out on duty.

At this moment Gildo came in, yawning.

What's up?

This lady can't prove who she is and she's looking for a man.

Ho, ho, ho – so she's looking for a man!

Only now did Gildo see Severina.

Ah, Severina. Yes, I thought you'd be along. I heard about Massimo. Well, what can I say, we all know Massimo. He'll be back. You just have to wait. Nothing we can do about it.

Severina, who was very agitated to start with, had been on the brink of a fit of fury in conversation with Adriano, but Gildo had calmed her down a little.

You could put out a Missing notice, though.

Oh, Severina.

I mean, you could look for him.

Suppose everyone whose husband goes off for a few days wanted a Missing notice put out?

Just so that we'd know where he is.

I wouldn't like to be working here then!

Severina stood there at a loss, fighting back her tears, and above all not venturing to look at young Adriano, who obviously enjoyed her useless pleading. She wasn't giving up yet.

The other three policemen returned from their errand, making a lot of good-humoured noise, joking and laughing as they came in.

Good Lord above!

The things we get to see!

Cheating on her old man, then she calls the police because he beats her for it.

Suppose all women called us out for that kind of thing!

And she'd been cheating on him.

Poor fellow.

To think what he suffered.

Cheating on him with the man next door.

He could have killed her.

Poor man.

He was in a bad way.

Severina, go home and wait.

And then she goes and calls the police into the bargain!

What does this woman want, Adriano?

She can't prove who she is but she's looking for a man.

Oho, looking for a man, is she?

So the signora's looking for a man, eh?

How about me, signora?

Or Gildo. He's a good man, is Gildo.

Stop it. Her husband's run off.

Run off, has he?

Gildo's wife would be pretty glad if he'd run off, wouldn't she, Gildo?

Stop it, I said, leave the lady alone.

We'll find you a man.

That's right!

Signora, it is the business of the police to find you a man.

What kind do you fancy?

Take a look at us, which do you like the best?

Severina, they're only joking, never mind them.

Severina! Hey, wait!

Never mind them.

I'd be off and away from that one too.

Oh, you idiots!

Gildo somehow felt sorry for her. Then she ran out,

weeping. Perhaps he ought to have gone after her to comfort her, he might even, for God's sake, let her dictate him a Missing notice. But then he could have ended up with a problem, he could be sorry. Massimo must have had some reason to go away, same as the man in Naggio had a reason to beat his wife. Well, we all know Massimo!

Weeping, desperate, hating these uniformed fools, Severina crossed the little bridge over the brook again. When she looked back, over all the rubbish in the water, she saw a face at the side window of the police station. A face in which all the malice and stupidity, all the arrogance and presumption, all the impertinence and fatuity of which a human being is capable were united.

12

Massimo stops again. It's hot, he wipes the sweat from his brow, sits down, he's in no hurry now, he is ready to postpone his homecoming, their reunion, the moment that for hours now he has been trying to imagine.

Oggia is over there. It lies sleeping. The sun is just about to move away from it. A young man comes puttering into the valley on a cross-country motorbike, on his way down to the village with a big silvery milk can on his back. Some people still keep sheep up there, and have to go up once a day to tend and milk the flock. The sleeping village of Oggia, which is full of voices and music only once a year.

On the patron saint's feast day the priest says Mass there. Early in the morning people arrive from all points of the compass, coming up from the village, over the mountains from Val Rezzo, from remote hamlets, often after travelling for many hours. For the last few years old Don Roberto and a few of the nobs have been brought in by helicopter. Its clattering sound tells the animals who usually have the village to themselves that this is no place for them today, and the wind it raises makes the young women hold down their skirts, while the old ones hold down the tablecloths on the festively laid tables. There is just room for the women and children inside the church. The men and the young people stand about in groups in the meadow, talking, smoking and already looking greedily at the long tables where bread and cheese, salami and ham and wine await them. Musicians fit their instruments together, more and more guests keep coming up the path from the village, greetings are exchanged, there are happy cries, surprises, embraces, voices that sound foreign, for on this one day in the year the former inhabitants of Oggia come visiting, those who emigrated thirty years ago or more to Alsace, where they all found work in a factory, since there were no jobs for them here. They bring their children, who don't understand the language of their native land, and the parents have often forgotten it themselves and can't get the hang of it again until they are singing the familiar old songs. Most of them will finally come back to Oggia only at the end of their lives, for their family graves lie here, with the guarantee of eternal rest in their native soil carved in two languages on their tombstones.

It was on one of these feast days that he had first noticed her. The time was already getting on in the evening, the plaintive clarinet melodies were still playing, drifting down to the valley, and those who had not yet started back home, intoxicated, were dancing, drinking, singing, talking, staring ahead in melancholy wine-induced mood, or happily smiling to themselves. Children were sleeping on their grandmothers' laps or had let their tired heads sink to the table top. The young men and girls thronged around the dance floor, courting, flirting, smiling shyly or boldly. Their time had now come, the couples and the families had given way for their courtship games. Massimo was the most brilliant, the boldest, the bravest among them, and close to him, dancing with him frequently, never taking her eyes off him, was Anna, daughter of the joiner Alessandro from the neighbouring village of Borgolo. A fine couple, said the older people, see how well they look together. So had Massimo thought too, at first, for he was proud of this conquest, and before long no one disputed it with him. But Anna was playing her own game and others, for instance Franco-Francone and Bruno, had already seen through it. She's waiting for her fairy-tale prince to come, they said, and until he turns up she'll take whoever she and many of the other women think the finest figure here. Somewhere beyond the mountains, however, there's bound to be a far better man. She'll end up with nothing, many people said. That's been known before, oh yes, that's been known quite often, people can name names, and they do, because arrogance flaunted so obviously will be punished, they're sure of that. Massimo soon felt the painful effect of Anna's moods. Sometimes she drew him close, then she pushed him away. When he threatened to move away himself she knew all kinds of tricks to lure him back. But in the process what Massimo thought he had felt for her was lost, and that was love. His ardour was extinguished. Whole days often passed when he never thought of her, when other matters seemed to him more important. He kept his distance from her, and more and more frequently her enticing gestures and calls were lost in the void. Anna became a pretty shell to him. She bored him. He was already looking around for other women as he used to, indulging his preference for sturdier girls, dancing now with this one and now with that, saying pretty things to them all, making promises, expressing little desires, loving without falling in love again, feeling a kind of sense of liberty, a sense of flying such as only he knew.

As for the pretty things Massimo said to the girls, causing them to smile with rapt attention and turn their eyes up to heaven, transfigured, so that they would look round for him with desire and whisper to their girlfriends, amidst much blushing, Franco-Francone could make nothing of it at all.

What exactly do you tell them?

Whatever comes into my mind.

Oh.

That's right.

So what does come into your mind?

I look into their eyes, and then I think something up.

Like what?

It's different every time.

Oh.

It depends on their eyes.

Ah.

I mean it depends on what I see in their eyes.

Listen, I fancy Roberta.

You do?

And when I'm dancing with Roberta and I look into her eyes, I don't see anything I could say.

Well, there's nothing you can do about that.

No?

Probably not.

Right, you tell me what to say to Roberta.

Tell her how much you fancy her slim figure, her long slender legs, her delicate face, that kind of thing.

At this point Franco-Francone usually looked at him with an injured expression, and the others laughed, because if there was one thing you definitely could not say to or about Roberta it was that she had a slim figure. She was the opposite: plump, round, heavy, and that was just why Franco-Francone loved her, knowing for certain that it would be a tragic mistake to have some skinny goat of a woman lying in his bed and living with him. What Franco-Francone finally said to his Roberta, what if anything he read in her eyes and what words he found to express it, well, no one knew. But anyway she became his wife, and Ferruccio the blacksmith reinforced their marriage bed with iron struts.

Anna, who knew she was a beauty because she was courted more than any other girl, couldn't stand it when a man rejected her and the favours she so graciously conferred. Then she would go on the warpath, and today was one of those days. That afternoon she contrived to be near Massimo all the time. She smiled, seemed pensive, sensuous, passionate, she sought his gaze, she indicated that she was there just for him, she gave everyone else the brush-off, she cooed and purred and scarcely left Massimo room to breathe. She danced more wildly than ever, when they were surrounded by darkness and the dim lights she kissed him more wholeheartedly and passionately than usual, she hung around his neck, he was the only man for her. He enjoyed the fight she was putting up, for he sensed that she couldn't rekindle his desire. It was too late. He looked over her shoulder as they danced, noticed who was coming and who was going, who was on the dance floor and who wasn't, who was dancing with whom and in what way. He saw the shy girls, the wallflowers, most of them sitting longingly on the benches, clutching their handbags and watching the dancers, dancing too in their own minds, counting the steps, smelling the sweat, divining something of the passion of the dance, and thinking how they would lie awake that night. It was the same for many of the young men too. They all watched Massimo, sometimes flying around fast and looking like a vivid carpet pattern, sometimes putting ideas into their minds for a moment when he danced slowly.

Severina had black hair, dark eyes, thick eyebrows, very white skin and slightly flushed cheeks, and her round face suggested that she was not particularly thin elsewhere either. Massimo was sure he had caught her looking at him. She shyly looked away, but he caught her at it a couple more times. He smiled, she blushed, and whether it was because of the resistance he was putting up to Anna, the wine, or some idea he took into his head, Massimo thought he had fallen in love with her. Who was she, where did she come from?

Anna went to sit right beside her when the dance came to an end. Bewildered and excited, Massimo went over to the men, found Franco-Francone, and asked who the girl next to Anna was.

Oh, that's Severina.

Who?

Severina. You must know Severina.

Her sister?

Her sister, that's right.

Ah.

Yes.

That's really Severina?

Well, she's grown up too.

Yes, I see.

Massimo left him and went to get some wine. Pensively, Franco-Francone watched him go, summoned up all of his intelligence that had not yet fallen victim to the wine, and thought: poor Anna. Yes, the arrogant are left with nothing in the end. Then he went over to Roberta, asked her for the next dance, and said something to her, but as mentioned before, no one ever knew what it was, because the clarinets were playing too loudly for anyone to hear.

Massimo watched Severina sitting beside her sister, who was imperiously ensuring that she herself was the centre of attention while the other young women and girls hung on her lips, envying her. Severina did not seem to hear her sister's increasingly hectic chatter at all. She sat there as if she were deaf. But it seemed to Massimo that her body was making circling movements, very gently, expressively, absorbed in the music. Once again his glance met hers as he stood leaning against a tree with a glass of wine in his hand, never taking his eyes off her. He smiled. She replied with a smile of her own, but so brief, shy, anxious and inquiring a smile that Massimo threaded his way through the tables and went over to her. Anna saw him coming, beamed, and naturally assumed that he was coming to ask her for this dance. She was about to stand up when she saw him take Severina's hand, raise her to her feet and step on to the dance floor with her, without so much as a glance for Anna.

The clarinets were singing now, were voices rather than musical instruments, the wine made the dancers sway, and the moon that had risen over Oggia, still misshapen, outlined the mountains and trees like a zigzag scissor-cut, inflaming the dancers' emotions. Massimo led Severina vigorously through the dance, whirling her around so fast that she felt the sky, the moon and the lights, the faces and the house walls merging into a single colourful pattern, and the blood rose to her head. He felt her abandon her slightly plump figure to him entirely, he looked into her dark eyes for a moment, and he fell in love. After that he danced every dance with her, and Anna was not the only one to be watching the pair of them, although she watched them with a fury that she could barely conceal. When her attempt to appear indifferent failed, she announced that she was leaving.

By now Severina was lost to her dancing partner heart and soul. She didn't know what was happening to her, or how it had happened. In the shadow of her beautiful sister who made all the decisions, as usual on such evenings, she had been thinking despondently of the end of the party, which would leave her alone as always, lying wakeful and excited in bed, and now here he was, drawing her into the centre of attention, where she had never been before.

She was silent, he did the talking. He told her how he lived up on a little farm in summer and worked as a woodcutter in winter, chopping wood for the pizzerias down by the lake with Franco-Francone, Albino and the other men. He told her that his grandfather had been the brother-in-law of those two idiots who hanged themselves from a hook in that house over there on the same evening, that he occasionally guided tourists who came into the bar up to the peak from which you could sometimes but not always see the Madonnina on Milan Cathedral, and how last year he had soared over the whole valley on the cableway with the dog on his shoulders, yes, he had flown like a bird. She smiled, but said nothing, not even that she knew all of this already – from Anna.

Then she was suddenly snatched away from him. Anna had finally decided to go home, and the bewildered Severina followed her. She smiled at him once more and then was gone. Only with difficulty did Massimo manage to join in his friends' endless drinking spree through what remained of the night. Franco-Francone, who hadn't shifted his massive body again after his two dances with Roberta except to make water against a tree or behind a house from time to time, understood what had happened to his friend. He put an arm around him and began singing.

Next day Massimo went to see Severina's father Alessandro the joiner in his workshop in Roncolo. The thin little man was standing at his bench gluing two planks together. He didn't look up but went on with his work. He knew Massimo by his voice.

I have to talk to you.

Alessandro carefully fitted a screw-clamp in place.

I have to talk to you, Alessandro.

You said so before.

I have to –

You have to or you want to?

It's about your daughter.

Of course.

I mean, that's what I wanted to talk to you about.

Go on, then.

What do you mean?

Nobody's ever known where he was with her yet.

I don't think you understand.

Oh, so I don't understand? You come here, you want my daughter, and I don't understand?

It's about Severina.

What?

Now, for the first time, Alessandro looked up from his work and saw that Massimo seemed to be very much in earnest.

About Severina.

Alessandro said nothing, stared at his work, took a damp cloth and wiped away the surplus white glue.

Well, well, so it's about Severina, is it?

Yes.

Fancy that.

What?

I suppose you know your own mind.

I do.

And I expect she knows hers.

Massimo said nothing.

Nor did Alessandro. He carefully fitted another screw-clamp in place, and six months later Severina and Massimo were married. Anna did not come to the wedding.

13

Massimo! Massimo!

Someone had rung the door-bell. Imperiously, firmly, and several times. Then came a call. A familiar voice calling Massimo's name in his sleep. Was it a dream? He woke up.

Renata was standing at the window, looking down.

There's some man or other down there. I don't know him.

What kind of a man?

I told you, I don't know him.

Let him be.

He's shouting your name, can't you hear?

She went into the bathroom, as if it were none of her business. Massimo didn't have to look down. He knew who it was standing there, and he knew the man wouldn't leave until he had told him, Massimo, what he had come to say. He would stand there like a tree, waiting, putting down roots. He had come a long way to do what he had in mind, and no one would succeed in driving him away. Massimo wouldn't escape him. He knew what the man had to say. Just as he had brought Anna and her children back from Bergamo because her husband beat her, now he had come here, dogged and determined, without making a great fuss about it, to fetch Massimo home.

Massimo!

The man was standing in the middle of the yard, a small,

thin man wearing a green hat and a dark suit, legs apart, steady as a rock. He looked up at the windows, saw people who did not feel he was addressing them gazing down at him, and listened unmoved to the angry slamming of windows and the occasional shouted request to shut up. That did not deter the man. At regular intervals, long enough only to say half an Our Father, sing the refrain of a song or utter several of the latest curses, he called out Massimo's name. His tone gradually became sharper, his voice louder and more menacing.

Massimo!

Massimo hurried into his clothes, glanced in the mirror, smoothed his hair. Renata came back from the bathroom, muttering crossly, and crawled into bed again.

Who's that?

Massimo didn't answer.

What does he want?

How should I know?

Go on down and tell him to keep quiet, dammit.

Then an idea suddenly occurred to her. She sat up in bed, smiled very slightly, with a trace of derision, and said: Aha, he's come for you! Is that it? Has she sent someone? Who is it? Her father?

What business of yours is that?

Massimo went out and down the stairs.

Massimo!

So he'd come, he had sought out Massimo and found him. Exactly how would remain his secret. At first, when Massimo himself wasn't sure if he'd be staying here, how long the affair with Renata would last, whether he could stand it here in the city or whether a longing for his familiar world would overwhelm him, he had been expecting her father to come for him. He hadn't. Now, almost a year later, there he stood, shouting his threat up at the buildings, a threat consisting of a single word: Massimo!

He did not move from the spot when he saw Massimo appear in the doorway downstairs. He just made a small, commanding gesture, and immediately Massimo realised that this man was not going to leave without a promise, without clear words and a decision. He slunk submissively over to him like a dog, playing for time, wondering what to do now. How was he to counter implacability in the person of a thin little man?

Alessandro took not a step towards him, did not offer his hand, showed no sign of recognition, pleasure, greeting. As if he had a perfect stranger before him, or a dog who depended on him and must be given orders, he said what he had to say.

So here you are.

How did you find me?

Everyone leaves a trail.

Massimo said nothing and thought of Severina, wondering whether she knew that her father would come here to fetch him home. And he thought of that quiet, simple, industrious man in his joiner's workshop, he thought of the sad and lonely Anna, whom this same father had fetched back from Bergamo, he thought of his mother, who had probably been sitting outside the house for the last year looking down the path along which he would reappear some day. He thought of Severina again and whether she would really want him back. And he thought of Franco-Francone and Bruno and Ferruccio, and Rosanna too, and of the farm up on the mountainside, the trees and the sheep and the damn peaks above, from which you could see the wretched Madonnina. Out of the corner of his eye he saw Renata leaning out of the window upstairs to watch the spectacle of his humiliation by Alessandro.

You wanted her that time, and I gave her to you. But not

so you could abandon her for some tart and leave her up there on the mountain with your mother, freezing to death or going crazy one of these days, or both.

Alessandro, I –

Hold your tongue! If I want you to say anything I'll tell you so. But there's nothing for you to say, so bloody well hold your tongue.

He spoke in a loud, clear, determined voice, a voice you wouldn't have expected from such a small man. It echoed back from the walls of the buildings. More and more people had begun to feel inquisitive, were looking down into the yard, wanted to know what was going on, what was up with the farmer that young woman had brought back with her.

You made my daughter Anna unhappy when you threw her over. She'd never have married that cretin from Bergamo if you hadn't trodden her love underfoot.

But I –

Hold your tongue, I say! You wanted the other one, I gave her to you. It wasn't easy for me. But I tell you, before you make her unhappy too, or crazy, or how do I know what else, you'll be a dead man. No, hold your tongue, dammit! By all the saints I can think of, by every last one of those damn saints, you're going back to your wife and your mother! Understand? And hold your tongue.

Massimo looked at the ground, couldn't look at Alessandro any more, and didn't want to see the faces of the people at the windows either. He stood there like a schoolboy caught in the act of wrong-doing and facing chastisement. He couldn't think of anything to say, any justifications or objections. Because he knew this man had a right to do what he was doing. Not only did he have the right, he *was* right. This wasn't Massimo's proper place. He must leave, must say goodbye to Renata, abandon her. He belonged at home with his wife and his mother.

He suddenly felt a pang of fear: suppose he never saw his mother alive again? She's old, he thought, she could die any time, she's so small and thin. She's drying up. And I am all she has left. She loves me. Yes, he thought, I must go.

I came on my own this time. Because I believe you'll see sense and do the right thing. I believe you can put an end to this business with the tart. I'm giving you two weeks. If you're not back where you belong by then, I'll be sending my sons. You know them. They don't go in for talking, you know that too. And if you don't, then ask that cretin from Bergamo. He'll tell you.

And Alessandro turned and went away. He stopped again briefly at the gateway of the yard, to look up at the window from which a woman's loud, scornful laughter rang out. Furious, Massimo went into the building, ran upstairs and into the apartment, tore Renata away from the window, covered her mouth and dragged her over to the bed, ready to lay into her. She laughed and laughed, and he became more and more furious.

But still she managed to turn his fury into wild passion easily enough.

14

What is it? Is this the same panic that seized upon her when she realised he'd gone? The same uncontrolled reactions that she won't understand later? What is she doing here? Why did she go over to the bird-cage, open the door, and shoo the birds until even the last made its helpless way out into the open? Why did she snatch the bedclothes off the bed, bring the wedding photo with her, and the gun? For she has brought the gun up here with her, up into the tiny loft, that triangular space above the kitchen that has been her refuge from the old woman all this year, her comfort, her nest. Like a heavily pregnant cat driven by anxiety, seeking the safest place away from the dog and the farmer to give birth, she kept creeping in here, as if guessing that some day she must go to ground in the loft.

She crawls forward to the skylight, which is no bigger than the palm of her hand, looks out, sees him. He can be clearly recognised now. She is lying down, you can't stand upright in the loft, breathing hard, distressed, hunted, an animal in flight. She feels the cold, smooth metal of the rifle barrel. The rifle again! What is she planning to do with it? Shoot him? She, Severina? Could she? She has never fired a gun, even in play. Even when they went to the fair in Porlezza, and Massimo put the rifle in her hand and encouraged her to fire it, even then, when it was just a case of firing at a little white pipe under a coloured plastic rose, she didn't dare. Trembling, she gave him back the gun, and he laughed and shot her down a whole bouquet of flowers.

Would she hit him from this distance? She rests the barrel in the skylight, presses her right cheek to the butt, that's how people do it, she's often seen them, men at the fair or on television. She doesn't think she's ever seen a woman do it. She looks through the telescopic sights on the barrel and at first sees nothing. She closes one eye, and now she sees a hairline cross against the blue sky. She moves the barrel down and sees the mountain tops, the bushes where she was working just now, the path along which he will come – the picture shakes – boulders, stones, grass, suddenly a pair of legs, a man's figure, Massimo. Her hand trembles, and with it the hairline cross, then she sees the mountain peak again, the sky again, Massimo again. Her hand grows steadier, her heart is not thudding so much; it soothes her to know she could do it, she has his life in her hands. Slowly, she follows his progress, sometimes with his head in her sights, sometimes his chest. The heart is on the left. If she pulled the trigger now would he be dead? She doesn't know. Is the gun even loaded? She feels the trigger with her forefinger. That's the place, that little hook, that's where you decide between life and death. Why does she hesitate? Can't she do it? Could she do it more easily if it wasn't a human being in her sights but an animal – a hare, a sheep, a fox, a wild boar – or just the little white pipe underneath the plastic flower? If she shot him now would she be a great avenger? Would it be his well-earned punishment for the loneliness and shame his desertion caused her? Would it make any difference to her memories of the scorn and derision she has had to suffer, and the look on that carabiniere's face, and having to listen to the old woman's reproaches? No, she'd still have all those memories. They would lock her up as a murderess, and bury him in the graveyard down there next to innocent little Sebastiano, and she wouldn't even be able to pray beside the grave and bring fresh flowers.

She puts the gun aside. No, there's no reason to shoot a man for going away for a year, whatever made him do it, particularly when he may be coming back full of remorse. There are other weapons, other ways to show how she despises him. She will continue to keep silent. Her silence will be her weapon.

Is he really coming back full of remorse? Does he feel repentant, is he homesick, does he feel a sense of longing? What for? For the old woman down there, his mother, who lives only to see him return, for the farm, the animals, the people in the village, his friends and their hunting together, for Rosanna, for his birds – or for her? Why is he coming now, of all times? Has her father carried out his threat to track him down and bring him back from Milan, Germany, America, wherever he may have gone? She would never find out from her father, he won't talk about it, he's not a man of many words, he does what he thinks he ought to do without wasting time talking about it. Like when he brought Anna home.

After deciding that no man here was good enough for her, Anna had married a short, fat sales rep from Bergamo. She moved into his parents' home, had two children, quarrelled a lot with her mother-in-law and in the end with her husband Alfonso too.

One day, when Severina was there with her mother, they had discovered that Alfonso beat Anna. Severina told the family at home. Her father said nothing, but next day he was gone, he'd caught the bus to Como, no one knew any more than that. A day later he came back with Anna, no longer radiant but sad and bitter, and the intimidated children and all Anna's possessions. Anna stayed. When Alfonso demanded a divorce and custody of the children because his wife had wilfully left him, Anna's father sent his two sons to Bergamo. After that Alfonso agreed to a divorce without custody.

The brothers said as little about their visit to Bergamo as their father did. That was how the men in their family had always been, said their mother.

Here he is, quite close to the house. His hair is longer than it used to be. He calls to his mother and begins to run, laughing. If she had fired the gun just now she would never have heard that laughter again, never have felt his rough hand on her skin again, or his breath on her neck. All that she has dreamed of in the long winter nights up here would be gone. And he would never know that she has become mute on his account.

15

The way she is sitting outside the house now, the old woman, ready to take her beloved son in her arms next minute, is the way she was sitting when Severina came back from her desperate search of the village and her visit to the carabinieri, humiliated, small, disappointed and lost. There she sat with all her reproaches, her derision and her scorn. They ate in silence, and between them stood that son, the magnificent, infallible, Christ-like son, the only one left to his mother, the son whose actions she not only understood unreservedly but also sanctioned, bestowing her maternal blessing on them. And since the silence that had suddenly fallen between the two women kept them safe from all that would have made it impossible for them to live together up here, they preserved it. There was nothing to say, everything had been said too often already, too loud. Even their looks, gestures, the inevitable movement of their hands said too much. This silence was an entirely new feeling. Simply to say nothing any more, to forget the words that describe things, if possible, isn't that a conceivable way of life? Severina liked the idea so much that she not only stopped speaking to the old woman, she spoke to no one else at all, not even to the Lord God at first, the Lord in whom she once used to confide so much, and to whom she prayed as she came back from the village where she would certainly never go again, asking him to spare her this shame and send her a merciful death. She would hang herself from the cable, grab hold of a branch, or just grasp the cable in her bare hands and plunge down into the depths, flying and flying until the cable chafed and tore her hands and she finally fell. She didn't do it, she dragged herself on.

Now she found strength in silence, relishing the words that were not spoken, although they still existed in her head as pictures of things. The pictures were quite different from the words you spoke. Down in the house in the village in winter, she often used to switch the television set on while she was doing housework, mute the sound and let the pictures into the room. They were usually pictures of the same things, ham, noodles, furniture, liqueurs, coffee, chocolates, cars, holidays. But when these things spoke to her just as pictures, not words, there came a point when she forgot the words that went with them and gave the pictures her own meaning. They were lovely pictures. Pictures of hawks carrying bottles up into the mountains in their claws to show them to their chicks; pictures of people with new furniture in their rooms who sat on the very edge of their sofas to spare them, telling other invisible people what beautiful furniture they had, and saying the other people ought to come and visit them, sit on the edges of the sofas and talk about the beautiful furniture too. And there were people flying across the mountains in cars, riding into space on noodles, landing on Caribbean islands among a crowd of good-humoured people. Pictures had always been more important than language to Severina. When Massimo first spoke to her at that party in Oggia, she had already formed such a clear picture of him that she was startled by the strange sound of his voice. It was as if she were predestined to live without language one day, and she had now reached that point in her life. She did not speak any more.

*

Franco-Francone came up bringing provisions, wine, salami. Severina did not speak to him. He shouted at her, shook her, spoke angrily to her, almost hit her, he was beside himself. Big, heavy man that he was, he was close to a heart attack, red in the face and trembling. A man who found talking so difficult himself, who had to dredge up the words from the depths of his body, groaning, in order to get them out at all, he now talked and talked and talked to her.

Severina, you'll go crazy.

Oh, by all the pig-gods!

You're crazy, that's what.

Just because a woman's husband runs off, that's no reason to go crazy and stop talking.

Many women would be glad if their husbands made off.

Do you think mine would shed a tear for me? Or stop talking? Stop talking! Ha!

Say something. Say something, will you, anything! Can't you speak? Are you sick? Shall I fetch the doctor up here?

Tell me! Tell me! Tell me!

He shouted at her, then turned to the old woman for support, looking as if he might join her in her air of triumphant suffering, but Severina signed to him, took him into the stable where the goats were, and kissed him on both cheeks. Bewildered, he picked up his things and hurried off, went down into the valley to tell them all about the mute, crazy woman up here.

She always was crazy.

Said some.

She never did say much.

Said others.

And Franco-Francone went around looking transfigured, with Severina's two kisses burning his cheeks even in his sleep. He would go up there again, he certainly would. Whether she talked to him or not. He would write notes, ask if she had lost her voice, if she ought to see a doctor, if she was ill, and what she meant by kissing him. And he'd ask whether she was lonely. Well, of course she was lonely, alone with the old woman, that poisonous, malicious old woman. Franco-Francone wouldn't be able to stand her company for an hour himself. And Severina was without a husband. Without a husband like Massimo, that fine man, the most wonderful husband anywhere, no one would have expected her to land him. Massimo who had really wanted Anna, but she turned him down. She's another crazy one, no husband now on account of her pride.

Yes, thought Franco-Francone, what's a woman without a man? Nothing. She goes crazy and forgets how to talk. Would his wife who talked all day long be the same? Would she go mute too if he left her? He didn't think so. No, Severina up there is different from all the rest of them.

He'll go up again. Tomorrow, the day after tomorrow perhaps. She'll be missing a man now and then. It's a funny thing, the women who have their husbands around all the time don't need them for anything but daily jobs about the house and farm, for taking orders, as material for news, rumours, chatter, scolding. But women whose husbands have run off or died, or women who never had a husband, long for a man until you can hear their sighing all over the valley. Did Severina desire him, Franco-Francone? Was that why she kissed him? Was it a sign? Dare he approach her in that way? Would words of love make her speak again? There'd be nothing wrong about it. The more he wanted it, the more he persuaded himself it was positively his duty as a friend to look after Severina for Massimo, and Massimo would forgive him. In fact Franco-Francone felt sure he would thank him. Thoughts somewhere between happiness and anxiety, thoughts he hadn't had for a long time, haunted him on those nights when he gave himself up to them, lying wide awake beside his wife, who came to this bed only to sleep on her back and snore until morning, which she greeted by sighing: Oh, is there never any end to this? Whether and when anything at all would come to an end – life, work, the year, the course of time itself – was not a question that ever entered Franco-Francone's mind. So far as he was concerned, everything in this earthly existence boiled down to two facts: a full glass and an empty one. And as long as he could empty the full glass and fill the empty one without too much trouble and expense, he felt the world was all right. He had made good, he was a woodcutter, he always had work, he had won his wife Roberta without much difficulty, the ideal wife for him, since her 120 kilos made her the only woman he knew who came within 10 kilos of his own weight. He had got Ferruccio the blacksmith to reinforce the bed with iron struts, he had given Roberta two daughters in it, and they were now teenagers who would soon be needing specially made iron bedsteads of their own. Life went on, and years ago he had given up expecting his own body and Roberta's to make any effort apart from working and eating. Something had fallen asleep in him, but Severina had woken it with those two silent kisses. It had disturbed him, and now made him lie wakeful beside his sleeping wife. Feelings ran through his body in a way that nothing but wine did usually, he sensed them in his guts, his heart beat fast, his head raced in free fall across a starlit sky. Outside, Fernando's gouty dog barked its elderly complaint into the night. Then there was a shot, and all was silent. Franco-Francone went to sleep.

16

Massimo runs the last few paces. There she is, sitting on the bench outside the house. She has fallen asleep. He stands before her, looking at her. Her head has dropped sideways to her shoulder, her almost toothless mouth is slightly open. Does she look older? He doesn't know.

Mamma!

She wakes with a start, but immediately realises who has spoken, spreads her arms wide, stands up and falls into his. Tears of joy come into her eyes, she is whimpering rather than speaking.

My boy!

Mamma.

My Massimo!

Mamma.

Here you are!

Yes, here I am.

And will you be staying?

Yes, Mamma, I'll be staying.

You mustn't leave me any more.

I won't leave you.

So you did come back. Bruno said you were coming back. But that was a long time ago, and then you didn't come back.

I'm here now.

My Massimo!

Mamma!

As he is still holding his mother close – she will not let him go – and feeling her bony body, he looks over her head in search of Severina. She is nowhere to be seen. She must have known he was coming. He struck the cable. She'd have heard it. Not his mother, she was asleep, and she doesn't hear too well any more. What did he expect, though? To see her standing beside his mother, welcoming him with open arms? No, judging by what Teresa and Rosanna have already hinted, it will be only his mother who welcomes him home at the moment.

Where is she?

The old woman immediately looks triumphant, and whispers in conspiratorial tones.

Up in the loft. She's stopped talking.

So I heard.

Nothing. Not a sound for a whole year.

Yes.

Come in. You must be hungry.

In a minute.

He goes to the stable, looks inside, sees the large pile of wood stacked outside the shed, the freshly painted rabbit-hutch. Everything is in perfect order. She has done it alone. She hasn't needed him. Not only has she survived a winter up here with the old woman, she has kept the little farm going.

He passes the bird-cage. It's empty, the door in the wire netting is open. She was always against those birds, she's let them out. Most of them won't have survived. He stops, bends down, sees fresh bird droppings on the ground. She has only recently let them out, when she knew he was coming, after he struck the cable to announce his arrival. An act of revenge.

This isn't going to be easy.

She doesn't need him, perhaps she doesn't want him any

more. Then what? Will he go down to the village with his mother and leave her to her own devices up here?

Come along, you must be hungry.

His mother is inviting him in from the doorway.

He goes into the house.

The old woman has already begun laying the table for him, just for him. She shuffles round the room with difficulty, putting wine and a glass on the table, bringing sausage, bread on a board, a piece of cheese.

You must be hungry.

Yes.

We spent all winter up here.

So I'm told.

I survived only because I knew you would come back.

And I have.

She is whispering, as if to prevent Severina up in the loft from hearing anything. Massimo has been doing just the opposite from the start. Everything he says, his questions, the tales he tells are meant for Severina in the loft too, intended as information, a message, an apology, meant to tell her: I've come back to you.

He looks round and realises that his chair is missing. His mother immediately knows what he is looking for.

She burnt it for firewood.

With every whispered remark she makes a small, malicious gesture towards the ceiling, rolling her eyes to heaven. Massimo doesn't know what to make of this yet, he doesn't yet guess at the feelings that have built up in his mother during this year, or how hard she will fight for him now, her son who still has his mother, a mother who has forgiven him, though his wife hasn't. Nor does he yet guess that, because his mother welcomes him back and takes him to her heart so unreservedly, it will take him much longer to come home to Severina. Such ideas are foreign to him. To him, a mother is a mother, a wife is a wife, they all belong under the same roof, it's only right and proper. He, who has succeeded in almost everything in his life, has mastered the most difficult of situations, even featuring as a hero at times, has not learnt that something once broken can never be fitted together again to make a perfect whole. Cracks and flaws will always remain.

So he presents his mother with the image of the master of the house come home, sitting at his own table. He eats and drinks, the wine loosens his tongue, and his loving mother hangs on every word that passes his lips. He tells tales of this, that and the other, brags, tells lies, makes things up, for no one here will doubt a word he says.

He talks about the Madonnina in Milan, she's as tall as the whole church down in the village, he speaks of the millions of pigeons in the square outside the cathedral and how flocks of them settled on his shoulders, of wide streets and magnificent buildings, street festivals and carnival processions, airports with huge aircraft, rich and famous people. And his mother beams.

He doesn't say why he had to go away for a year to see these things, what part that woman played, what he was doing all that time in Milan, what he was living on, whether he was working, where he lived, or why he has come back now. His mother doesn't ask. She just smiles blissfully at him, overjoyed, and falls asleep in the middle of his stories, exhausted by happiness.

He picks her up. My God, she's light as a feather. He lays her on her bed, covers her up, sits at the table, drinks, looks round the room, up at the ceiling, wonders whether to try going up, whether to call to her, speak to her. He can't decide what to do, he is afraid. He goes out into the yard, where he is overcome by a wonderful sense of pride: I am back where I belong!

He takes a couple of steps, turns round, looks at the house, the darkening sky above it, stars, the peak of the Madonnina.

One of these days I'll blow that peak up.

He thinks.

17

It was autumn, and life in the city was less and less comfortable, which made Massimo think of home more and more often. He finally realised that he was homesick. Depressed, he shuffled through the falling leaves in the wretched little park at the end of the street and thought of the colours of the hills, the leaves of the forest trees, the steely blue sky above them, the shining lake. He sat in the café with doddery pensioners who talked about their fear of not seeing the winter out. He was out of work again, and survived the days only because Renata came home to him at the end of them, kissed him, pulled him to his feet and out of his dreams, and dragged him off into activities for which his idleness all day had made him too tired. She never rested. If she wasn't working she wanted to be out and about, having fun, in bars or at parties. There was always something going on, she was always being invited somewhere. When he happened to have casual work himself she went alone, coming back some time towards dawn. He was jealous, imagined her with other men. They had quarrels which she thought quite unnecessary, for she didn't, she said, know the meaning of faithfulness. They quarrelled with increasing frequency, which made him realise more and more clearly how much he wanted his old world back.

How long had he been here now?

Two months? Three? He didn't know. He had gone away in summer, and now it was autumn.

They'll be having those fine, clear days outside when the mountain tops stand out against the sky in a saw-toothed outline, when you see the 'Teeth of the Ancients', as they call the mountains, more sharply than ever. In this weather you can easily see the Madonnina on Milan Cathedral from the mountain peak. How far is it from here to there? Seventy kilometres? An hour by car, two by train and bus. He could go, thought Massimo, maybe at the weekend. Go out there, go into the bar, see Franco-Francone, Bruno, Albino, have a couple of drinks, tell them about the new and different life on which he'd decided to embark. It would be like when people who had moved to Como or Milan years ago occasionally turned up in the village. They soon felt at home again, the place was familiar, they recognised everything, thought there hadn't been many changes. But they brought a touch of something strange into the bar, it was as if they were taking photographs of their old life for the family album, so that they could show their grandchildren in the city the place where they grew up. You could tell that they were wondering whether they would want to live here again. You said a cordial goodbye, and felt glad they had gone. You opened all the windows wide to let in the mountain air.

But if he went back, that would be quite different. After all, he was from the village. Or was he still? Would it really be so simple to go into the bar, chat to friends for a while, and then disappear again?

What would he tell them? Could he do such a thing to Severina and his mother? Wouldn't he have to go up the mountain?

No, there was no chance of such a visit now. He must stay here or go back for ever. He knew that if homesickness drove him back then it would be for good, so he didn't go.

But soon after that, when they had quarrelled, he went to the station, bought a ticket and boarded the Como train. He got out again just as it was beginning to move, went back, upstairs and into the bedroom, and into Renata's bed.

How warm she was, and how delicious she smelled! And how she relished his defeat!

I'm all right.

Don't worry, Severina.

You must shear the sheep now.

Get Franco-Francone to help you.

You'll be going down to the village soon.

I'm all right.

Don't leave going down too late.

Get Franco-Francone to drive the livestock down for you.

Get Albino to slaughter a couple of animals.

Don't worry.

How's Mamma?

It's just the way I am, you see.

I can't change myself.

Are you both all right too?

I hope so.

Regards from Massimo.

Regards from your Massimo.

See you soon.

Massimo.

See you soon.

Your Massimo.

Regards to you both.

See you soon?

He meant to write a letter. Or a postcard. A picture postcard of the Madonnina. He had bought one in the cathedral, but he didn't know what to say. He had never written a letter in his life, and the postwoman would read any postcard first.

See you soon.

Your Massimo.

See you soon? When? When would that be? Did he intend to go back? Should he, could he promise a thing like that?

I'm all right.

Was he all right? Yes, with Renata sometimes. But more and more often he was not all right. Then all those thousands of thoughts and ideas that added up to homesickness came back to him. In his mind he got up with Severina in the morning, drank his coffee, crumbled bread into it, fed the rabbits, drove the sheep to another part of the pasture, mowed the meadow, chopped wood, lit a fire in the hearth, roasted a joint of meat, slaughtered an animal, sheared a sheep, took the fleece down to the valley, did some shopping, went into the bar, talked to his friends, spent the night with Rosanna, climbed up the mountain again next morning, told them the news from the bar, entertained his mother with a few jokes and gossip about the villagers, got into bed with Severina in the evening, took her in his arms, made love to her. It all seemed close enough to touch.

And when he walked through the city, when he sat in the café with the old men and listened to their tales of their life here in the city, it was as far away as America, a place from which no one came back, where people spoke another language, where they used quite different words for things and didn't understand people from other countries.

Let's go to America.

Said Massimo.

What would I do there?

Asked Renata.

America would be final, he thought. It wouldn't allow him to feel homesick.

*

America. America. America.

He said it to himself three times.

Like Uncle Gusto in the past, his father's brother. They called him the American. He was the only person Massimo knew who had ever come back from America. As a young man before the war he had sold his house, his land and all his possessions and gone to America with his wife. Soon long letters arrived from Colorado. They'd struck lucky, they really had struck lucky. The letters became fewer and further between, shorter, didn't mention luck any more, finally there was a card from New York: Paola died yesterday, regards from your grieving Gusto.

After that nothing, no sign of life. The war came and went, the post-war years washed many stranded people up on shore, Massimo's father came home with the war still in his head, no sign of life from Gusto. No one thought he could still be alive.

One day there was a beggar at the door, holding a note out to Massimo, who was a boy at the time.

Gusto Brunetti from America.

There he was.

Massimo ran in to his mother with the note. She recognised her brother-in-law at once. He had come back, he was alive, but he was mute. They gave him a little room in the attic, and he stayed. A slightly built, grey man of just fifty who looked ancient. Unable to do any work, he sat all day on the bench outside the house, or in the kitchen or the shed, just staring ahead of him. He was looking at something somewhere in the distance.

I wish I knew what he sees, said Massimo's mother.

There she was with two men in the house, one of them still with the war in his head and always shouting, the other with America in his head and always silent. The many notes that Gusto scribbled told them what he wanted to say at the moment, but they never found out what he had done in America. He wrote down too many American words that no one understood. Malicious tongues said that Gusto could have talked all right if he wanted, he just didn't want to so as not to have to tell people what had happened to him. Massimo often sat in front of him trying to guess what was written on the notes, and he didn't understand how anyone could manage not to talk if he really could. He tried it himself, and couldn't keep it up for as much as half a day. Sometimes he suddenly asked his uncle questions, trying to trick him into talking. It was only at such moments that Uncle Gusto smiled. When he died, he apparently said the same word loud and clear at the end, three times:

America. America. America.

Now that Massimo too often sat around doing nothing, he thought of his uncle, and with his own doubts he felt close to him. America didn't really mean anything to him, he could as easily have dreamed of Australia or Asia, for he imagined that all he had to do was put a great ocean between this new life of his and the old one. But suppose he came back to the village some day like his uncle, shabby, poor and mute?

He didn't write a letter.

He didn't write a postcard.

He was homesick, but he couldn't go home. He was unhappy, and comforted himself with his good moments with Renata, but they were fewer and further between, and took place almost exclusively in bed.

I'll go back at the end of the year, he told himself. Christmas came, the city was full of bright lights, it was cold and he couldn't find work. He was living on Renata's earnings now. They quarrelled more and more frequently, shouting, hitting out, only to fall into each other's arms and hold each other close again. He became increasingly aware that she had no one either. The people she called her friends were pleasant, agreeable, passing acquaintances who were interested in her only when she was feeling all right, cheerful and ready for anything.

Snow fell even in Milan in the New Year, and Massimo found temporary work with a snow-clearing gang at the airport. His workmates were south Italians whose dialect he didn't understand when they talked to each other. All that linked him to them was homesickness. They had lives of their own where they came from. They wanted to go back and were dreadfully cold here, but they couldn't go home, because there was no work for them there.

Spring came. Massimo kept putting off his decision to go back. Every quarrel with Renata could have offered the opportunity. He couldn't do it, and by now he was afraid to. He was at the station again one day in March. There was an hour to go before the train left. He took a note out of his jacket pocket, where he had found it a few days ago. It was a piece of paper on which he had scribbled the number of Bruno's mobile. He called it from a phone kiosk.

Hi, Bruno.

Who's that?

Massimo.

Hey, where are you?

Milan. The railway station.

I'm in Schaffhausen. Are you coming home?

Yes, the train's about to leave.

Great. I'll be back myself in three days' time.

See you, then.

I'm glad you're coming back. Everyone needs you. Time for that adventure of yours to come to an end now. I mean between you and me, Massimo, I can understand it, always did, but not for so long, no, no.

I'm coming back.

Massimo hung up, opened the door of the kiosk and went out. There stood Renata, small, sad and tearful. She jumped up at him, just as she had at the start, as if he were a tree she wanted to climb.

She kissed him.

18

Severina lies awake up in the loft for a long time. She has put the bedclothes over the trapdoor and is lying on it, so that no one can push it up and open it from below. She hears every word, hears his breathing and the old woman's happy chuckles. She hears when he pours wine, when he drinks, when he cuts a slice of ham or breaks a piece of bread. And even when they are whispering down below, obviously talking about her, Severina can hear it, because there is only this board between them.

She never says a word any more.

I know.

How do you know?

People are talking about it.

At first she thought she couldn't bear knowing he was so close but not seeing and feeling him. But nor could she simply have confronted him. Running away might be another possibility. However, the longer she lies here, listening to him talking and laughing, the calmer she feels. She is close to him, closer than for a long time, but the curtain of all this year's suffering hangs between them. It protects her. Severina notices very clearly that his boastful narrative, louder than is necessary for the old woman, who is not really very hard of hearing, is meant for her too. He is bringing her into it, telling his tale for her benefit, he is impatient and wants to pull the curtain down. The ordinary incidents which he makes into adventures, something he does very well, are meant to be his apology. That's his style. And the whole story of that woman, and the woman herself, will slumber on in the most remote corner of his heart, and they'll have to take very good care not to awaken her there. He is bringing her, Severina, into it, telling her his tale too. Massimo, as Severina senses from up here, is back again as if he had never been away, as if he had simply been spending a day in the village. Just like a man, thinks Severina. Men's words make light of what has happened, turn injustice into justice, hold the victim responsible. She, Severina, will now be the guilty party, the one who doesn't go straight back to normality, who protests, who still remains mute. For Massimo, the world will soon be back in order. He will shear the sheep, repair the shed, kill a hare, keep his mother sweet, and lay claim to Severina's body. And he will return to his old ways. He'll go down to the village again and again, and everything will be back to normal.

He will go briskly down the mule path, he won't stop at the bend where a little plateau offers a view of both lakes, he will make for the village and pass the first house, Luigi's. But it won't be just as it was before, when Luisa always contrived to be doing something at the window when Massimo came down the mountain, so that she could give him her slightly foolish, longing look and smile at him. No, Luisa will be sitting in a dark room, praying and repeating Valerio's name to herself over and over. Valerio, Luisa's son, who had an accident in a trial of courage and did not survive.

The trial was to ride the boys' highly tuned, noisy motorbikes up the mountain along the mule path to the top station of the transport cableway, and then down again as fast as possible. After the bend, which you had to take slowly so as not to be thrown off the track there, Valerio had accelerated again and was crossing the finishing line at the entrance to the village when he tried to throttle back his engine, and was thrown off the bike right outside his parents' house. He died at once, his skull smashed in. Luisa saw his death, for she was doing something at the window. There is a memorial niche in the wall protecting the path on the mountainside, where an ever-burning light and fresh flowers remind everyone that Valerio set a record which no one has broken since. Franco-Francone has told Severina about the graveyard, Valerio's skeleton and the yellow jacket, and about Luisa who is no longer crazy, but very quiet and sad. She won't contrive to be doing something at the window just as Massimo is passing any more.

He will go through the arch of the gate, down the few steps, past the public wash-house. Oh, if the women happen to be there! Maria-Grazia, Gabriella, Rosanna, fat Violetta and toothless old Mother Guaita. What a lot of chatter there will be, what competitive cackling and cooing, what a polyphonic look-who's-here, full of secret desires and daily disappointments and sighs from TV love stories. Oh, how well Severina knows it! And how proud she has always felt to think that this man, whom you all admire, for whose love and favour you all burn, is mine, just mine, and you all envy me for him. A woman who attracts such envy will harvest even more derision. Severina has discovered that in the last year, when she came down and called his name all round the village, imagining him everywhere and nowhere, in this woman's bed or that woman's bed, but he wasn't with any of them, and nor, as they crowed out loud over the wash-tubs to the gracious sky, nor was he with her, the deceived, the betrayed, the crazy one, and after that the silent one, the mute woman.

Massimo will go on passing Franco-Francone's little house, and Franco-Francone will be standing at his door, hands in the huge pockets of his shapeless dungarees, in his mouth a cigar stump that went out hours ago. They'll go to the bar together. Franco-Francone will talk about the wood he has cut with Bruno today, which will be just the same as the wood he cut yesterday and the wood he will cut tomorrow. Or perhaps he will talk about yesterday's wood instead, but only because he didn't cut any today but has been slaughtering a pig with Gusto. It will have been a wonderful, marvellous pig, because to Franco-Francone, who knows no greater pleasure in life than the consumption of sausages and ham, the pig he has just killed is always the best pig he ever slaughtered. The pleasures of anticipation ennoble the pig. There will be tales told of it from the house to the square, where they will meet Gusto, who for his part will be able to confirm that this pig was indeed a very special pig.

Tell Massimo, go on, tell him.

That's right, yes, it was, oh yes.

What did I tell you?

An excellent pig.

Yes.

Just like I said.

That's right.

Okay, I believe you both.

Gusto's my witness.

I am that!

Fine.

There'll be children playing in the square, young girls leaning against the wall talking, surreptitiously looking under their lashes at the boys riding motorbikes over the square, doing tricks for the benefit of the girls, of course, who else? The men will be standing round the bowling alley, talking shop, calling out to each other in encouragement, pouring scorn, everyone knowing better than anyone else. One of them will call to Massimo.

Massimo, hey, whose bowl is closer?

Alberto!

And they will laugh, because everyone will know Massimo has no idea which of the bowls is Alberto's, but it will be their way of saying ah, here you are again, and his way of saying yes, look, here I am again. They will talk about him too – the way they did about her – whispering, guessing, perhaps even secretly despising him. Not that such things will matter to him, it'll be all one to him. And there, thinks Severina, is the difference between him and her, perhaps the difference between man and woman in general. He knows they all know that he's come back, but his wife is still mute and hasn't returned to her marital duties. Franco-Francone will have told them that. Massimo will know, but he'll strut across the square like a king. That will silence the talk, stifling any scorn and derision. If he were to ask which is Alberto's bowl they'd tell him, but his authority would be lessened. Of course they will bow to his firmly pronounced decision that Alberto's is the closer. Paolo, who was sure just now that his was, will accept the verdict. And with that Massimo, if he was ever away at all in the minds of the men, will finally be back in his familiar place in their world again – sooner than he will be back in his place with her, and just as well for him, thinks Severina. Because there they will listen to his stories, expressing amazement or agreement.

Then they'll go into the bar. Teresa will already be standing in the doorway, greeting him with her usual ceremonious curiosity.

And he will tell his tales, and they'll hang on his lips, and should any of them quietly have blamed Massimo for his behaviour he will energetically dismiss the idea. For he brings them the adventures they don't have themselves. He lets them join in.

No, there will be no one there to condemn him, and

Rosanna will happily take him back into her bed too, forgiving him before he has even touched her.

And she, Severina, will have nothing left but her silence. She knows that she will not speak again until he is really suffering, until he doesn't see it as just the moodiness of a woman scorned, until he has understood that it is he who brought this silence between the two of them. For a whole long year. The time will come when he has told all his tales and he too wants only to be silent. She senses that, for she can hear him down there now, grateful for his mother, a hearer who is devoted to him, basking in her admiration, resting in her love, full of high spirits, letting his stories take flight – stories which, surely, are only a fraction of what he has really experienced.

19

Few people thought much of it when Severina stopped coming down to the village. They were sorry she had turned mute, and a little surprised too, but not at first really astonished.

She never did talk much.

Said Bruno.

What would she say?

Said Franco-Francone.

If he comes back she'll soon start talking again.

Said Teresa.

What would she talk about to the old witch up there?

Said Albino.

Franco-Francone had given up trying to talk her into anything. He carried her up the shopping she had written down on a list for him, sat there for a while with the old woman, who was delighted to have someone to talk to, and let slip no opportunity for a dig at her silent daughter-in-law. He brought the village news. In this family a baby had been born, in that family someone had died, a calf had perished, someone had been run over, fallen ill with cancer, been cuckolded by his wife or fallen into the brook dead drunk. There were other, more important news items: Rinaldo's wife had run off with the Sardinian cook from the pizzeria down by the lake. The proprietor of the pizzeria had dumped his Ferrari Testarossa so as to get the insurance,

Gildo on the supermarket sausage counter is probably gay and so he won't be employed by the supermarket any more, Luigi took Holy Communion last Sunday with his flies open, to the amusement of the entire congregation, and young Adriano Rossi the carabiniere's mother has died. Talking away thirteen to the dozen and suddenly falls down dead.

That's the baker's son?

Yes, Adriano the baker's son.

He's dead too.

That's right, and the son is another Adriano.

They're related to us somehow.

Said the old woman.

That's right.

How, though? I don't remember.

Anyway, she's dead too now.

He's a carabiniere?

That's right, down at the police station.

Just fell down dead, did she?

Talking thirteen to the dozen.

Fancy that.

She always did talk a lot.

Yes, so she did, so she did.

Some women talk too much, some talk too little.

Or not at all.

Or not at all.

Which do you think is better?

It would be better for my Roberta if she didn't talk so much.

This was how their conversations usually went. Franco-Francone had to repeat a lot of what he said, or repeat it in a louder voice, because Amabilia didn't catch it, or had forgotten it, or wanted to hear it again. Franco-Francone enjoyed watching Severina at work. She didn't show whether or not she was listening to the conversation. And at the very back of his mind there were feelings he dared not betray to her, not that she gave him any opportunity.

In two weeks or so, said Franco-Francone, he and Albino would come up here, kill the beasts due for slaughter, and help them drive the others down. Severina looked up in surprise, saw his uncertain gaze and the old woman's venomous expression, and walked away.

Surely she's not planning to stay up here through the winter?

With her, you never know.

We can't let it go that far.

She doesn't say anything anyway.

Then winter came. It announced its advent with the first frosts and with snow, which at first the sun melted, then with icy winds howling around the house and the rocks. The animals were cold and restless in their stalls. The men came up before the first really deep snow, determined to offer their help, trying to talk Severina round, warning her, losing their tempers, expressing misgivings, finally deciding that Severina had probably gone crazy and they would at least take the old woman down. But she refused to go with them.

What would I do down there all alone?

You'd be warm.

And who'd cook for me? Who's there to cook for me?

Maybe Rosanna.

Said Franco-Francone.

Ha! Her! It's partly her fault he left!

So they left empty-handed. Franco-Francone promised to come up with provisions if there wasn't too much snow on the ground.

Then they were gone, and it was quieter than ever.

Winter came in, so hard a winter that even the sounds in the air froze to silence. It was a long time before real snow fell, yet snow would have been kinder than the frost, snow to wrap itself round the house and warm the roof, snow that Severina could have melted for water to wash in. As it was she had to break off the icicles into which the spring had frozen, a laborious task, and thaw them out in the fireplace.

The little radio set told them when it was Christmas. When she heard the first Christmas carols Severina switched it off. A day before the Christmas holidays Franco-Francone had come up with some biscuits baked by his wife, arranged on a paper plate with a Christmas pattern. Severina gave him back the plate.

On Christmas Eve Severina could not sleep. She wrapped herself in her thick quilt and went out. It was a cold, clear night with stars in the sky, and Severina had to fight off terrible sadness.

The birth of the Lord.

What was he born for?

She asked herself.

She could find no answer.

When she went indoors she was surprised not to hear any snoring or groaning or whimpering from the corner where the old woman slept. She went to look; the bed was empty. She went into her own bedroom, but the old woman wasn't there. She went out again, tried calling, and realised for the first time that her throat would not make a sound. She found the old woman in the stable, lying fast asleep among the sheep, warmed by their bodies.

Severina refused to look at this as a peaceful Christmas scene. As she saw it, it was only the old woman's obstinacy.

After Christmas, just in time for the New Year, the real snow came. Severina had nurtured secret hopes that by the end of the year Massimo would have thought better of it and would come back. With the coming of the snow, removing them as it did so entirely from all signs of life down below, she abandoned those hopes. Not even Franco-Francone would come up now. Now they were completely isolated. They both felt it, and as if they had always liked each other, as if there had always been a close friendship between them, they moved together. They warmed themselves by the hearth, side by side, and listened to the melodies sung by the wood on the fire, the old woman too silent now. Long before Severina was tired the old woman fell asleep, slipping off the fireside bench, and Severina had difficulty getting her into bed. Once there she sighed briefly, a sigh that turned to loud snoring that you would hardly have expected from her frail body. Severina usually sat there much longer, thinking about her life, which appeared to her useless, unnecessary, not worth preserving. If I died now, she thought, it wouldn't matter. No one would really miss me. Yet she felt so much alive that, out of all her many thoughts, she always took ideas of desire to bed with her.

New Year's Eve was another cold, starlit night. The old woman was already asleep, it was midnight, and Severina trudged out into the snow. Bright, colourful bangers were going off in the valley. Severina thought of the first firework show of her childhood. A large crowd had gathered down by the lake. She and Anna and their brothers were there, with their father. There was going to be a firework display on the island in the lake, the same as every year. That year it had rained heavily for the last few days, and no one was at all sure whether the firework display would be held. Then they heard it was to go ahead after all. The crowd, after scrambling for the best places, waited two hours for it to begin. Severina was perched on her father's back, feeling very excited. A fanfare sounded, the signal for the show to start. Nothing happened. The crowd grew restless and began to murmur. Finally there was a bang, a single rocket flew about twenty metres through the air, hissing and pulling a yellowish-red trail of light along behind it, and then came down to earth. A loudspeaker announcement said that unfortunately the firework display would have to be cancelled this year.

Well, there we are, said her father.

They set off for home, but they didn't get far, because ferocious brawling had broken out ahead of them. The angry crowd was attacking the organisers of the firework show, everyone was punching everyone else, no one knew who was on which side, they were all just hitting out at random. War must be like this, thought Severina. From her secure position she watched the fight. Her brothers were having fun urging the combatants on. The fight lasted longer than the firework display usually did.

Best firework show I ever saw, said her father that evening.

The colourful flower-like fountains rising in the sky grew few and far between, now and then there was a last bang in the distance, and then silence. Severina looked up at the starry sky. She felt warm and at peace. She lay down in the snow so as to see nothing but the sky above. It covered her with its many lights like a warm blanket.

She fell asleep, and flew. She was flying over the valley on Massimo's back, clinging to him. She felt his breath, sensed his strength, heard the whirring of the cable, saw heaven and earth fly past, she was flying. They were flying, and it would never stop.

Trying to die, oh yes, that would just suit you!

The old woman was hitting her with a stick. She had come out of the house, seen Severina lying in the snow, marched over to her.

Confused, Severina stood up. What had happened? Had she fallen down, had she fainted? Dazed, she went indoors.

Only when she was in bed did she realise that she had been in heaven, with little Sebastiano.

Why didn't you leave me there?

20

No, Massimo won't be reconciled to her silence. This can't go on, it must change. This sort of thing doesn't happen. After all, he's come back, he's promised not to go away again, he's admitted he was at fault. If she had run away, told him she didn't want to live with him any more, that would have been different. Or if she had ranted and raged, hurling angry words at him, he could have taken that, but remaining mute, simply mute, being there, doing her work, the two of them eating from the same dish, shearing a sheep together, sitting together at table but in silence, he can't take that much longer. She had better go. He can't live with a mute woman. She is mute because she hasn't forgiven him. To think of all the ways he's tried! He has set traps in the form of sudden questions. He has talked to her. He's told her stories, all the stories he has already told his mother. He talks all summer. He thinks that he has never talked so much in his whole life before. He talks to break the silence that he cannot endure. And if he wants to hear human voices, needs conversation, he goes down to the village. He goes more often than he used to. Sometimes he comes back up the same day, sometimes he stays down there overnight. He used to notice that she always felt slightly suspicious of that. Now she seems entirely indifferent to whether he stays down below or comes back up the same day, whether he has news to tell or says nothing. Sometimes he has the impression that she isn't listening to him at all, she has given up listening as well as talking. Once she wanted to know everything that went on down in the village, and she was the one who set traps in the form of questions, asking after various women, mentioning their names as if by chance. He always had to be on his guard. She never asked after Rosanna.

The probing questions of the village people are beginning to spoil his trips down the mountain. They are inquisitive, particularly the women.

How is she?

How do you think?

Is she talking yet?

Mhm.

Do tell us, Massimo, is she talking?

What business of yours is that, Teresa?

I was only asking.

You'd do better to keep your mouth shut.

Oh, dear God, I hear she still isn't talking?

Mother Guaita, it's better for her to keep quiet than talk such nonsense as you.

That's women for you, thinks Massimo. You have to let them talk and not bother about it, or else tell them something to stimulate their imagination, stir them up, something they can pass on to other people whether or not it's true. And what about the men? They don't ask questions. They're torn between envy and pity for someone with a mute wife. She'll talk again some time. The main thing is she's doing her work and otherwise she's normal. The men still admire Massimo and look up to him. He is still the centre of the company at the bowling alley or in the bar, just as he used to be. By telling them all kinds of true stories and quite a few more that he has invented, Massimo has managed to interest them in his return, making them feel that they too have shared in his year of adventure. They don't ask after his wife, they can all remember her, after all, and only occasionally, late in the evening, does Massimo let slip a few scraps to satisfy the curiosity of the last drinkers, suggesting in a mysterious and, to many, a puzzling manner that there's a very different kind of woman who is something special, but she'd destroy a man if he stayed with her. Intoxicated, they agree that such a woman must be a fire on which a man could singe his wings like a moth. This observation sends them home to their conjugal beds more satisfied and content, although no fiery sparks fly in those beds now. And Teresa, the one woman who is witness to such conversations, passes restless nights in her own bed upstairs when she has closed the bar after the last of them have gone, the bed visited by her husband Andrea only at weekends to sleep off his hangover. She dreams of Massimo coming in and lying down beside her.

Massimo is on his way down to the valley yet again. Rounding a bend in the steep downhill path, he sees the rooftops of the village. Behind the jagged mountain peaks that they call the Teeth of the Ancients the sun is setting, bathing the lake in a light that makes it look like a large, oily puddle. Massimo passes the memorial to Valerio's sad speed record. Luisa is not standing at the window as she used to. All she does now, Luigi has told him despairingly, all she does now is sit on a chair in front of the boy's picture, weeping.

Beyond the arched gateway of the entrance to the village, Massimo sees a woman getting out of a car. It is Anna. He has already heard that she came to live here not long ago, alone with her children. Once her brothers had married there was no more room for her at home. He hasn't seen her since his return. She is plumper now, there are grey strands in her blonde hair, small folds have formed around her mouth, folds that seem to Massimo evidence of the grief she has known for years now. She's still beautiful, he thinks. Perhaps because she isn't so proud any more. None of the arrogance that had been turned full force on Massimo seems to be left.

Anna!

Massimo!

Why, wonders Massimo, why don't we greet each other with two kisses on each cheek, the way old friends and relations do? They shake hands awkwardly. Later on, Massimo will know why. It is the sense of unfinished business between them, something yet to be done. He himself has never really thought of it. But now here is Anna, standing before him like a monument to their missed opportunity.

So you're living here now.

Yes, I'm living here.

Alone?

Yes, well, alone during the week. The children go to school in Como. They're only here at the weekend.

Ah.

Like I said, I'm on my own in the week. Call in some evening when you're not going back up.

He does not reply. There's a touch of her old recalcitrance about her again, her demanding, arrogant manner. Yet he sees that she is not the Anna of the past. She is embittered, lonely, and at the moment she is persuading herself she wants something she once passed up.

You'll be welcome any time.

Yes, well, now that you're living here. We'll see.

It could be there's something you want and it'll send you to me.

No, not now.

How can you say that when you want everything you see?

I don't want you. That was over long ago.

That's only what you think.

You know it was.

I know what I see and hear.

What you see and hear gives you no power over me.

Who knows?

I do.

You do?

Yes.

There they are, those remarks from the past, the gestures, the smiles, the seductive manner, the scorn. Massimo guesses, but will not admit, that Anna is threatening to draw him into her fine-spun web again. The web where lust and pain chase each other. Hasn't he just been suffering that for a whole year? Get out of here now, quick, he thinks.

And you'll call in some time.

Well, yes, we'll see each other here in the village, our paths will cross.

She smiles, and suddenly presses close to him. He feels her body, smells her perfume, her breath touches his neck. Only for a moment. Already, intentionally or instinctively, she is withdrawing into unapproachability, and from that position she is enticing him.

Could be that you'd like to talk to a woman now and then too.

And she's gone.

He looks after her. No, she can't disturb his life any more after so many years, a life just returning to normal. He doesn't want any complications now, any dramas, any new entanglements. Only what's close to hand, what's familiar and can be picked up where it left off, for instance Rosanna.

Outside his house stands Franco-Francone, hands in the huge pockets of his shapeless dungarees, in his mouth a cigar stump that went out hours ago.

Let's go to the bar.

Yes, let's, why not?

We killed a pig today.

Anna's living here these days.
We killed a pig, I said!
I just met her.
Gusto and I slaughtered it. A good pig.
She's on her own now.
I haven't slaughtered a pig like that in a long time.
Alone with her arrogance and everything.
Here comes Gusto. Ask him yourself.
But that's life.
Gusto, tell Massimo about that pig.
An excellent pig, that was.
Like I said.
You don't get to see a pig like that every day of the week.
Fine animal.
That's right.
Yes, that's right.
You can say that again.
Yes.

They reach the square, where there is a leisurely, relaxed atmosphere. The men's voices can be heard from the bowling alley. Young men ride noisily across the square on motorbikes to impress the girls leaning against the wall, giggling and whispering and stealing glances at the boys under their lashes.

Ah yes, Anna.
Says Franco-Francone.
She's landed up here now.
She's grown old, too.
And all on her own.
Got her just deserts.
Hey, Massimo! Whose bowl is closer?
Alberto's!

Teresa is standing in the doorway. She smiles, and for a moment he thinks that if it were just a case of having another relationship as well as Rosanna to provide the village with gossip, he might fancy starting something with Teresa. As usual, she greets Massimo with her solemn curiosity. There is a touch of satisfaction about it today.

A few days ago Teresa called on Rosanna, wanting an answer to the question which is arousing burning curiosity, not just hers but the curiosity of others in the village too. Is Massimo seeing Rosanna again?

He is.

Proud and happy, Rosanna explained that her former lover was indeed visiting her once more. Remorselessly, straining Teresa's powers of imagination to the utmost, she described all the things Massimo wanted in bed these days, things that greatly enriched her emotional life.

About a month ago, in the corner of the wine cellar where Andrea kept his tools, Teresa had discovered a drawer full of well-worn magazines. The pictures she found in them helped her to imagine what Rosanna was talking about now, and led her to the conclusion that the woman Massimo had been living with in Milan must have been a tart. Rosanna was of the same opinion, and succeeded in convincing Teresa that it was the duty of a woman to act like a tart for her man, or the man would find one elsewhere. At least, she had read the same advice in several magazines, a kind of household tip for women sandwiched between lasagne recipes and the latest summer fashions. If women could act like tarts for their menfolk then the menfolk wouldn't go astray, that was the idea.

In that case he wouldn't be coming to see you!

Yes, he would.

But why, if he got what he needed from her?

Rosanna ended the conversation, in her own opinion, on a solemn note:

Ours is a true love story.

At any other time that would have made Teresa laugh. Now she was thoughtful as she went home, and for the first time after visiting Rosanna she wasn't wondering whom she could tell, extracting a promise of strict secrecy. She felt all churned up. She tried to remember the first time with Andrea. She began to feel ashamed of what had become of her sex life. What was left of it? Dreams, romantic ideas, and a sense of shame when she brought herself off without thinking of Andrea as she did it. And what does *he* do, she wondered, on the long weekday evenings in Switzerland? Do he and Paolo visit tarts, do they have girlfriends, were they really working in German-speaking Switzerland that time they didn't come home for three whole weeks, do they take women to the hostels where they stay? Or does he have to satisfy himself in the same way as she does, using these magazines to help his imagination out? Will we ever know what men feel, what they want, what they're like? Are Rosanna's accounts really just fantasies or stories she found in women's fiction magazines?

Men and women, said Rosanna, do things together we could never have imagined, not till now, but they're fun.

As soon as she was home Teresa went into the wine cellar, took out the hidden magazines and leafed through them. So that's what Andrea wants. She'll be like that, that's how she must offer herself to him, and then he won't drop straight off to sleep beside her. That is what he wants to do to her, and that's what she ought to do to him. And Massimo does this kind of thing with Rosanna. Did she want that? *Could* she do it? Wouldn't she feel ashamed, having to watch Andrea at the same time? Would it be easier with a lover, someone you didn't sit down with afterwards at table, eating and talking about ordinary everyday things, making practical decisions? Yes, a man like that, a man who came through the back door in secret by night for an hour or two in your bed, a bed warmed by anticipation, you could be different with him, perhaps you could be the way these pictures and Rosanna's tales say you should. But with Andrea? What would he think of her? Would he think she had been unfaithful and was insatiable? And could she really do things like the women in those pictures, letting men put anything they liked into their mouths, black or white, rooting about inside themselves with slender fingers ending in long red fingernails, presenting themselves to men in positions that Teresa would have been totally incapable of assuming? The pictures did not excite Teresa as much as Rosanna's stories. They hurt her, tormented her, pursued her. And yet things must, could, had to change somehow.

When Andrea came home from Switzerland on Friday afternoon the bar was closed. He was surprised. He hurried into the house calling for Teresa. No answer. She was not in the yard or the bar or the saloon. He went upstairs and opened the bedroom door. There she lay, naked but for a suspender belt, with red lips, red fingernails. She was smiling and tried to pull him down on the bed with her. He stared at her, ranting and raging.

Are you out of your mind? Have you gone crazy?

Come here, Andrea, do come here.

Gone on the game, have you?

But this is what you'd like, Andrea, come here!

Good God above! My wife a tart! In broad daylight.

The magazines, Andrea, the magazines under your tools downstairs. I was looking at them. I wanted to be like that for you.

He strode out, shouting and complaining to all the saints he could think of, went into the cellar, grabbed the magazines, left the house, got into his car and drove away.

How can anyone understand men, Teresa wondered, surprised to find that she didn't feel ashamed, she didn't feel humiliated, instead she felt a growing certainty that now she was going in search of a lover.

She got up, removed her makeup, dressed, went downstairs, opened the bar, and that evening she looked at the men in a new and different way. But she didn't fancy any of them. The one she would have liked to see most wasn't there anyway.

Andrea came back late that night. He lumbered upstairs, drunk, and fell on Teresa without the least consideration for her, just the same as every Friday night.

This time she didn't shed tears afterwards.

Massimo and Franco-Francone go into the bar. There are a few men playing cards, some others are standing by the bar counter, talking.

Hi, Massimo.

Hi. Hello.

Down here again, are you?

Yes.

Any news?

Is she talking yet?

Damn it, don't you have any other problems to think about?

Only asking.

We're worried.

No, she is not talking.

Perhaps she can't any more. I've heard of that kind of thing. Your voice suddenly goes. Like going blind.

The usual questions and answers, the usual discussions and anecdotes, a sad and no longer talkative Luigi, and then there's Teresa. Massimo notices that she looks different from usual. She has painted her nails red. She never used to do that. She is looking at him, trying to catch his eye so that she can smile at him. Oh my God, no, thinks Massimo, not with

Teresa. Everything's back to usual with Rosanna, and that's all right. She doesn't talk about it, she keeps it to herself, their familiar ways matter to her too much to be broadcast all round the village. Is there some connection between Anna and the change in Teresa's manner? Is Teresa thinking: now that Anna's living here she'll get her claws into Massimo again, so I'll get in ahead of her? Is that the way women think? Yes, of course women like Teresa think that way.

Thinks Massimo.

His self-confidence shaken daily by the silent Severina, he enjoys being desired by these other women. It does him good, he enjoys it, and while consuming increasingly large quantities of alcohol he responds to their courtship with meaningful glances. Yet he is not sure. Is this what he wants? With Teresa, whom he has known since she was born, and who, as the only woman in this bar, has always been off limits to everyone here. Teresa who had to marry Andrea because she was pregnant by him. As far as he knows Teresa has never had anything to do with another man. Knowing about other people's affairs was always enough for her. She knew far too much about the men here, she knew their weaknesses much too well, she wasn't so much a woman you'd have an affair with, even just a one-night stand, as a listener you could pour out your troubles to. Something must have happened to Teresa. Andrea didn't come home for three weeks. Is there something wrong? In her old age – Teresa is in her late thirties, with a daughter almost grown up – does she want to know what it's like to have a lover? Could she possibly know about him and Rosanna after all? Is she jealous? Does Rosanna boast of her lover to Teresa? Or is it in fact Anna's appearance here in the village urging her on? Massimo decides not to let himself in for this, although Teresa, as he has never noticed so clearly before, is really very pretty. She'd broadcast it all over the village, triumphing over Severina. He doesn't look her way any more, he avoids her eyes, yet he avidly breathes in the smell of perfume and sweat when she puts a glass of wine down in front of him, pressing herself slightly against him on the pretext of having to collect some empty glasses. No, he's not letting himself in for this, not now, not today. He will go home, or perhaps look in on Rosanna, who so passionately celebrates his return to her bed, which is no longer littered with dolls.

He is one of the last to leave the bar, with Bruno, Albino and Franco-Francone. Ciao, Teresa; See you tomorrow; a pee together against the wall in the square beyond the bowling alley; Good night, all – and they set out or stagger off on their way. Massimo looks back at the bar once more. Usually the light of the blue lettering saying *Bar Sole* goes out at this point. But Teresa is still standing in the doorway, watching him go. He waves, she waves back, he goes down the street and over to his house. There's a little light on in Rosanna's bedroom. She knows he is in the village and is luring him with that light, as usual. It's become a habit.

Massimo goes on, turns into another alleyway, and is standing – just how he doesn't know – outside the house where Anna now lives. The flickering of the TV set tells him that she is still awake. But he hesitates. Is this what he wants? It certainly excites him to think of her enticing him now, when she treated him so arbitrarily in the past, just as the mood took her. And she's still beautiful. But it is all so long ago, he has just come back to her sister Severina, and he didn't come back to cheat on her with Anna now. Who is he, so easily lured by these women, so willing to fall in with what they want? No, he'll keep Anna on a string. He'll see how things go in the immediate future. He is tired and slightly drunk. He will go to bed and sleep, and climb up the mountain tomorrow and tell Severina: either you start talking, now, or I'm going away for ever. He goes back along the street, turns out of it, follows a stray cat, comes into the square and sees the lights still on in the bar. Teresa is clearing up, washing glasses. Standing in the dark, he can watch her. She is washing glasses, the sleeves of her blouse rolled up, and you can see her breasts bobbing up and down. She has tied back her hair, but one strand is hanging over her face, and at that moment Massimo feels great desire for her, a lust for someone new, so close and so tempting. He knocks very softly on the window. And as if she had known he would come back, as if she were sure her courtship of him that evening would work, she opens the door, draws him in, puts out the light and holds him close. They don't talk.

How can anyone understand women, thinks Massimo hours later on his way home to his house in the village, as day is dawning behind the mountains. He followed a woman to Milan, he was ready to destroy his whole previous life, was captivated again and again by her body, and now, here, he discovers Teresa who will do all those things too, the things that always bound him to that bed in Milan. He is astonished, bewildered and overwhelmed. He doesn't want to think what will come of this, but he has a feeling that Teresa won't spread abroad what has happened between them. Poor Rosanna, he thinks, quietly entering his own house, you've lost your lover. The light in her window is not on now, yet he thinks a head has just disappeared behind the half-drawn net curtain.

Went to see that Anna, did you?

Rosanna hisses at him, snake-like, when he leaves the house with the pannier on his back later in the morning.

Did she bring it off, then?

He does not reply. Armed with the rights of a woman scorned, she plants herself in front of him.

Am I spared nothing with you?

Helpless himself in this situation, he leaves her alone with her sorrows and her misconceptions.

21

The train had come into the huge spaces of Milan Central quite suddenly. Massimo didn't really know how they had arrived, he hadn't seen anything on the way, hadn't been thinking of anything, hadn't asked himself why he was sitting here in the train with this woman and the four strangers. He had been drunk, confused and in love. He, who always did whatever he did deliberately, was so utterly bewildered, had given himself up so wholly to these five people whom he had known for only about twelve hours, that now, when the train abruptly stopped and all the passengers rose to their feet, picked up their things and made for the doors, he woke up to reality for a brief moment and asked himself: What for God's sake is all this in aid of, what am I doing here, what do I want, is this really what I want, what am I after here, what business do I have in this place?

With an unerring instinct for his doubts, Renata, who had never let go of him during those two hours in the bus and then in the train, the way you hold on to some valuable rustic antique brought home from an expedition into the country in case it gets broken or stolen, brought him back under her spell by jumping up, flinging her arms round him, pulling him to his feet, hugging and kissing him. Her souvenir, her trophy, the prize she won this weekend for climbing the mountain!

We're here!

Milan!

Come on!

How they had laughed and joked in the train! Renata's four companions, members of a small theatrical company, had sung songs, mimicked well-known politicians and entertainers, cracked all kinds of jokes and made faces. They imitated Adriano Celentano, Zucchero, Pippo Baudo, Raffaela Carra, Berlusconi, Dino Zoff, Schumacher and Barichello, Eros Ramazotti and the Polish pope in Rome. Massimo was drawn into the game too. He had to sing their songs, he told carabinieri jokes, and was asked several times to repeat the story of how he flew across the valley with the dog on his shoulders.

And it pissed on you.

Out of fright, yes.

I never piss out of fright.

I only piss for joy.

I could piss myself laughing.

So it really did piss on you?

Out of fright, yes.

I don't believe it!

Can't be true!

Who'd ever think it!

Can't be true!

Then, suddenly, he was alone with Renata in the huge, high station concourse, with its dimensions that made human beings look so small. The theatrical people had said goodbye with a wealth of words, gestures, kisses, they had to catch a suburban train, they fluttered off like a flock of tattered crows.

See you!

See you!

It was not the first time Massimo had been here in Milan station. He had been to a football match in the San Siro stadium with friends a couple of times, and he and Franco-Francone had once gone to an agricultural show where they were among the woodcutters competing. They had cut a disk of wood from a thick tree-trunk in eight seconds, and came seventeenth. He had not noticed the sheer size of the station then. They had been talking, surrounded by fans or by visitors to the show, thinking only of getting to the buses standing in the station forecourt that would take them on to their destination.

Now it was all different. The majesty of the station restored a little sense to Massimo's mind. He would say goodbye now. He might drink a last coffee with her and then catch the next train, and after that the blue bus going along the lake. He would shake this adventure off as if he were brushing newly fallen snow from his shoulders. He would be back in the village square in three hours' time, he'd go into the bar, boast of his new acquaintances a little to his friends, be back home where he belonged. And everything would be the way it ought to be.

Come on!

What?

Come on, do!

Where?

To see the Madonnina! The Madonnina on the cathedral!

She embraced him, jumped up on him, wound her legs round him as if he were a tree she wanted to climb, kissed him.

They walked on. Her little hand vanished in his.

How good she smelled!

They crossed the square with all its pigeons and went into the cathedral. They climbed the tower, and for the first time Massimo stood face to face with the Madonnina. She was no little Madonnina really, but a mighty golden Madonna five metres tall. It was she who brought me here, he thought. Did she know what she was doing?

Then they walked through the city, went a few stations on the underground, clinging to each other all the time, and ended up in Renata's apartment and her bed. They stayed there for several days and nights, and Renata felt that he was putting down roots.

Massimo often lay awake during those nights. The sounds of the city resonated outside, and every few minutes a plane flew over the building with a noise like thunder. These were the planes you saw from up on the mountain, flying at a great height, shining silver, sometimes leaving a streak of white on the sky. You knew that they were flying to Germany, and you couldn't hear them. Here in Milan, they took off from Linate a few kilometres away, and for about a minute each of them drowned out the turmoil of the city as it passed overhead.

How long had he been away now? A couple of days. He was alone with his thoughts for the first time. Renata had to go to work; she was a waitress in a bar. He could stay here in her apartment or stroll round the city. He was still afraid of getting lost there, passing thousands of people and knowing none of them, unable to greet or exchange a few words with anyone.

So he sat at the window, looked out, saw the piece of sky left in view by the gables of the buildings. A sky like a cleaning-rag. He saw housewives hanging out washing on little balconies, men in jogging trousers smoking, children playing in the yard.

What will Severina have thought, what will she have done, what will she have told his mother? At some point – perhaps yesterday or today – she'll have gone down to the village, looked for him in the house there, asked about him. She'll have found the remains of that night's feasting. Rosanna, complaining and jealous, will have been there with her. Severina will have felt fear and panic rather than jealousy. My God, he hadn't tidied away any of the traces. They left in such a hurry that the house would give it all away. The rumpled bed, the champagne bottles.

Come on, let's go down to the lake!

Renata had said.

In view of his deception and betrayal of them, perhaps Rosanna and Severina will have made common cause and consoled each other.

He'll be back.

Rosanna will have said, because she simply wants to think so, won't hope for anything more.

Does Severina know or at least guess at what's become a habit between him and Rosanna?

And then Severina will have gone looking for him, asking questions about him, all round the village. Oh, some of them will have said, so your husband's gone, well, fancy that. Yes, they will have mocked her, or at best comforted her. She'll have gone back up the mountain sad and confused. God, what has he done to her? She wouldn't be able to understand. After all, there'd been no trouble between them. No quarrel, nothing.

And the old woman, his mother, what will she have said? Her only son, the one person she has left, has abandoned her. How will she cope with that? Will she survive it? She is old, thin, small and frail. She could die any time. Perhaps she really will die of grief at his departure. It may be that he'll never see her again. He is all she has left. All the others have died. Her elder sons, her daughter, her husband.

What kind of a life has she had? Outbursts of fury from his father, who beat her. He beat Massimo's brothers and sister too. That was the war in him, they were powerless against it, and Massimo was too young to protect them. His father never beat him, he didn't know why. His mother always made allowances.

The war, it's the war. That's what the war made of him.

Massimo's elder brothers seemed to have inherited their father's impatient restlessness. They were regarded, like him, as crazy and unpredictable, and they did all they could to prove it. They climbed the tallest trees and church towers, they clambered up any cliff, they fought, they defied death. Young as they were, people feared them. They roared through the villages together on their motorbikes. They wanted to be racing drivers. They drove just one race, an unofficial, forbidden race organised by themselves.

They raced along the lakeside road to Como in a stolen car. Neither of them had a driving licence. When they crashed head on into a heavy truck they died instantly. That was the year when their father died, and Uncle Gusto died a year later. They were just seventeen years old, the twins Silvio and Rhino. A year later Massimo's elder sister Primina, who had been ill all her life, died at the age of twenty. Now his mother had only her youngest child, Massimo. And she felt, quite early, that his father's war lived on in him too, that he too was restless and uneasy. He was always challenging fate, and she feared what else fate might have in store for her.

She has lost so many to death, his mother, and now he has left her too. He's left behind two women who managed to live together only because he was there. It has often cost him a good deal of trouble to make peace between the two of them. His mother saw Severina as a scapegoat for all her own pain. She treated her daughter-in-law as if she, Severina, were responsible for so much unhappiness. Massimo knows that, but he has always closed his eyes to it. They rubbed along somehow or other. And there was a time when they really were all one happy family. That was when little Sebastiano was born, and had two mothers to care for him.

But Massimo's mother couldn't forgive Severina for the baby's death either, just as she will not forgive her now for her son's departure.

What have I done?

I've deserted them both.

It can't be right this way.

And what for?

For passion. Well, there's that at least.

But what was to come of it?

How was it all to end?

Could he spend his days just waiting for Renata to come back and take him in her arms?

Those arms, that smell, that body, this bed. Would he be able to do without it?

Wouldn't he need money? He'd have to look for work. But how was he to find work here in the big city? The unemployed sat in bars from early in the morning, staring into the depths of their glasses. There'd be no work for a farmer who had strayed into the city because of passion. Holy Madonnina, what have you done?

He knew he'd have to go back. He'd have to bring his adventure to an end, and at once. Adventures mustn't last long. They must be brief, and come to a creditable conclusion – like that flight of his on the cableway over the valley. He must get away from here. He didn't belong here. He was nobody here. He was just the latest in heaven knows how long a line of this woman's lovers, a woman he scarcely knew and of whom he knew nothing at all. This room, this bed, the dismal courtyard outside, the dirty sky, the noisy city, this woman, they couldn't be his life.

But they did become his life.

For then Renata came in, right into the middle of his thoughts, flung her aura of intoxicating perfume and seductive words around him, seduced him, was passionate and demanding, burrowed into him, sent him burrowing into her, robbed him of all his reason.

No, he won't go back, because he can't do without her any more. He was lost to her and to her life, a life that was still so strange to him.

22

Severina has not left the mountain again since her visit to the carabinieri. She didn't want to set eyes on the village any more, hear people whispering about her or pretending to be sympathetic, see the house where he had that orgy, or Rosanna and her open grief at Massimo's departure. Severina didn't want there to be any reason for her to go down again. Franco-Francone, Bruno, Albino and her brothers brought her the necessities of life, and all of them did it because they knew she'd rather starve to death up here with the old woman than go back down to the village.

There was only thing Severina wanted: her child's grave. She missed standing at little Sebastiano's graveside, praying for him. She invented a grave for herself. She put a crucifix and a picture of the baby in a niche in the rocks up above the house. That was where he now lay, or so she liked to tell herself. She stood or knelt there every day to pray. And of course she prayed out loud, for no one but little Sebastiano and the Lord could hear her. She could hear herself too. That was a comfort, for sometimes she thought she might forget how to speak entirely, might not know the words any more. Sometimes, when the fear of being truly mute tormented her in her sleep, she sat up in bed and said anything that came into her mind. That soothed her.

There was no reason for her to go down to the village. And now that Massimo is back he goes down regularly. She writes him lists of what she needs, and he brings it back with him. And while she never listened to the old woman's constant complaints, she does follow what Massimo has to say about life down there with interest. The village and its people are coming closer to her again, just as life in general is becoming more normal. Massimo has probably said everything he thought worth saying, leaving out the real reasons why he left. That's the way men are, thinks Severina. I'm back, they say, isn't that wonderful for you too, life goes on, let's carry on working together again, let's sit at the same table, lie in the same bed. But Severina will not do that last thing. Other than her silence, it is the only weapon she still has against his too-hasty overtures of peace. She can't, she doesn't want to, not yet. So when he goes down to the village he doesn't come back until next day. Rosanna has got her lover back sooner than Severina, who climbs up to the loft every evening under the old woman's scornful eyes. Even on the nights he spends in the village she sleeps up here in the nest that is hers alone. It is true that she sometimes lies awake hearing Massimo and the old woman snoring through the wall in competition with each other, and she feels a great longing to go down, crawl into bed with him, smell him, feel him. But for the old woman she would probably have done it long ago. But she will not allow her that further triumph. So they have been living together again for a month now, living past each other, against each other.

One day Severina comes down the ladder in the morning, goes to the kitchen sink, washes, puts water on for coffee, looks out of the door, sees Massimo mowing the meadow, lays the table, glances at the old woman's bed, surprised that she is not up yet, stops short, goes over, sees the old woman lying lifeless on her back, feels her pulse, crosses herself, and when Massimo comes in she points to the bed without a word.

Mamma, what's the matter, Mamma – is she dead? My God, how did – she's dead!

He looks at Severina, who nods.

Oh, my God. Pray, pray for her, Severina. She didn't have Extreme Unction, pray for her. Severina stands there, looks at the dead woman, does not move, does not fold her hands.

Massimo is running around in confusion.

Well then, I'll go down. I must fetch the doctor to certify her dead. And he goes. Severina goes to the door and watches him leave. He is sad as he walks away, afraid that there will now be eternal silence up here. Will he come back? Perhaps he'll send men to fetch the body and stay down in the village himself. What is there here for him now that his mother is gone? A wife who won't speak to him, won't share his bed. Perhaps they mock him on her account, and they will stop asking after her some time, a woman he doesn't need at all any more, since he has Rosanna and who knows who else. Anna, perhaps? She has moved into the village and Massimo has seen her, he told her so quite casually, too casually. After all these years, has Anna reached out her hands to take the man she didn't get in the past? He won't come back, thinks Severina, going into the house again.

There lies the old woman with a peaceful, contented expression on her face. At that moment Severina envies her. She held her son in her arms again, it was for that she resisted Death's wooing, and now she could give in and fall asleep. Severina sits down on a chair and talks to her.

So there you lie. You're the mute one now. And I am speaking. I'm to pray for your eternal rest, said your son. Your beloved son! He left me alone with you for a year. I had to listen to everything you said. Your reproaches, your complaints, your wailing and scolding. I couldn't do anything right for you, only your son mattered. You forgave him everything. He left us – not just me, you too! But you thought it was my fault. Your wonderful son can't be to blame for anything. My son, my son – there was nothing else for you. I was just dirt, the scum who took your son away from you. And you thought it was my fault that we had no more children after little Sebastiano's death. You aren't a real woman, you once said. That was just like you, malicious, you were a wicked witch. I wouldn't have wished you to see him come home. Yes, I wished you dead. And I don't feel guilty about it. What is your son doing now? Is he saying a single Our Father for you and your eternal peace? Isn't he just running away again? Do you think he'll put flowers on your grave? Not he, don't imagine he will. He never visited little Sebastiano's grave, never. Or the graves of his father and his two brothers who died in that accident, or his sister's grave. That's not men's business, praying and visiting graves. But you're in luck, Amabilia Brunetti. In spite of everything I will pray for your soul. Because I believe in eternal peace, and one shouldn't be at odds with the dead. That's the only reason. May the Lord grant you rest eternal.

She prays out loud.

Then, for a long time, she looks at the wrinkled face, the fixed eyes, still open, the thin grey hair. She does not see a beloved figure in front of her, just any old, dead person. That is how you look when you grow old, she thinks. You get wrinkles and hair like that, that skin, those liver spots, that furrowed brow and gaunt look, light down on your upper lip, the emaciated hands, the deep-set eyes. Never before has Severina been so conscious of old age. Never before has she so consciously looked at a dead body.

When her own mother died she was still a child and didn't understand what had happened, hardly felt her loss.

Slowly, almost solemnly, but fearfully too she draws the covers back from the dead woman. She has never seen an old person naked. She is alarmed, staring at that small white body. Pale, almost yellow skin over a skeleton and a network of veins, thin, tubular breasts, the old woman's hips, her grey pubic hair, her thin legs lying there like bleached bones, as if they didn't belong to the body at all, the folds of her neck, the wrinkled face from which the blood has long since drained, as it has from the whole body, the few thin hairs through which the skin of her scalp shows white. She covers up the body again, closes the eyes, as if in apology, folds the hands on the quilt. Then she goes out, sits down on the bench where the old woman always used to sit, and weeps. But her tears are not for the dead.

Will she sit here some day like the old woman, waiting for death? She won't have a son worth waiting for. If Massimo doesn't come back there'll be no one to wait for. No one else will come, she'll become as one with the wood of the house, she'll turn to wood, disappear, dissolve into nothing and follow little Sebastiano at last. At this moment she wishes for the death she had wished on the old woman a few weeks ago.

As a child, she thought you could hold your breath and then you'd die. She knows better now, and she envies the old woman indoors. She's managed it.

Massimo comes back with the doctor and his friends Franco-Francone, Bruno and Albino. They are carrying an empty coffin.

While the doctor officially pronounces the old woman dead and makes out a death certificate, the men stand in the yard, talking.

Yes, it's going to be quiet up here now.

Very quiet.

Poor Massimo.

I couldn't stick it.

It can't go on.

Listen, Severina, you have to start talking.

You have to start talking at last!

Who else is he going to talk to up here?
The sheep or what?
Severina!
It just can't go on.
I mean, he's come back.
Do see sense, Severina.
He doesn't deserve this.
Not now his mother's dead.
What do you think, doctor?
Is it normal?
I mean, she's sick.
In the head, sick in the head!
You talk to her, doctor.
Leave her alone.
But...
I mean, poor Massimo.
Leave her alone.
With his mother dead and all.
She will speak when she wants to speak again.
Says the doctor.
When will that be?
That's the question, you see.
Give her time.

Franco-Francone has gone over to Severina, looks at her, and putting his round, red, fat face very close to hers, he whispers:

You can speak if you want to, Severina. Can't you?

She nods.

Then say something! By all the saints, by the good Lord, say something, do!

Then she watches a curious funeral procession leave. Massimo and his three friends are carrying the coffin, and the doctor, the only one of them wearing black, brings up the rear carrying his bag. They disappear round the first bend, come into view again a few more times, and then finally start along the path down into the valley.

The coffin.

Franco-Francone said.

The coffin's heavier than the corpse inside it.

Massimo will stay down in the village to prepare for the funeral and deal with the official business. The funeral is to be in two days' time. For the first time in over a year Severina will put on her Sunday best and go down to the village. Her throat already constricts at the mere idea of it.

She is alone here. She's up here alone for the first time. It's a strange feeling, weird at first, then it becomes more familiar. She can lose herself in that feeling, she can hear the absolute silence and break it by shouting, laughing and singing. She laughs, and an echo comes back from the Madonnina mountain, she calls down into the valley, and is then alarmed in case the men carrying the coffin down can hear her. She sings the songs of her childhood, all the songs she can remember. Then the songs that only the men usually sing.

Bring me roses when I die, bring me roses for my grave.

Would anyone bring roses to her grave? Would anyone stand by her grave as she stands by the grave of little Sebastiano? Will Massimo visit his mother's grave? With horror, it occurs to Severina for the first time that the old woman will now lie beside or above Sebastiano, that whenever she goes there to pray the prayers will be for the old woman too. Well, she will keep them separate. She will tell God that her prayers for Sebastiano are for him alone. And she will say a prayer for the old woman in God's name. Or perhaps she won't go down at all. Why should she? To see the people who derided her, to let Massimo show them: look, she's here again, everything's all right now. Wouldn't it be better for her to stay up here for ever? She goes to the grave she has made for Sebastiano. She prays out loud. Then she goes into the house, takes the bedclothes off the old woman's bed, clears away all memory of her. There's a glass ball on the bedside table containing falling snowflakes and a little model of the golden Madonnina. Severina shakes it, puts it down, waits for the snowflakes to settle. Then she throws the glass ball into the fire. She opens all the windows, sits down on the bench again, and now – she can hardly believe it – she feels happy and content. She is all right.

She thinks of Massimo. He has no one but her now.

As for her, if she would only go to them and speak to them, breaking down the wall between them and herself, she would have her father, her brothers, their wives and children, Anna and Anna's children. But apart from some distant relations who will be coming to the funeral, Massimo's family has died out. His two older brothers were killed as teenagers in a car accident, his sister died young of cancer, his father died because of the war, or so the old woman always said. Others claimed he died of madness. Can't his madness, Severina wonders, have been because of the war?

Yes, she is now Massimo Brunetti's only relation. The silent wife who climbs up to the loft every evening. The wife who would so much like to lie in bed beside him, embrace him and kiss him, feel him, but who can't any more. It hurts her, yet here she sits now thinking of him with tender affection, and she believes that she is happy at this moment.

Will she still feel happy when she goes down the mountain tomorrow, walks behind the coffin through the village to the graveyard, stands by the grave in front of everyone who hasn't seen her for over a year? Should she go down at all? If I don't go down, she thinks, then he'll never come back again. Is that what she wants? *Can* she want such a thing? Can she live up here alone without him? Can she survive? Or would she simply lie down on the floor or in the bed, hold her breath, think of nothing and wait for death to take her? Would it be good to die now, she wonders? All the struggles, all the grief, all the disappointments that life has brought her and has yet to bring would be as nothing. Massimo could look for a new wife, perhaps a younger one who can still have children. Should she stay here and not go down so that he never comes back again and can begin another life? She can imagine just being dead. She lay down in the snow before, up here in winter, she went to sleep and would have died if the old woman hadn't brought her back to life. A thing like that can happen in winter. A kind, gentle death. She felt its touch at the time. It caressed her warmly, there was nothing cold about it. But how could she manage to die now, in early autumn? Hang or stab herself, shoot herself, throw herself off the rocks? That's suicide, she can't do that. The Lord God would never forgive her. Lying down in the snow and going to sleep, lying there asleep for ever, is the only death apart from a natural one that she would permit herself.

Forgive me, Lord, I was tired and I went to sleep in the snow. I had forgotten it was winter. Forgive me, Lord!

No, you don't die as quickly as that in summer. So she will just stay here. If Massimo doesn't come back then she'll starve to death sooner or later. She won't slaughter any of the animals in order to survive. And at some point winter will come, bringing the first snow.

The part of the graveyard that slid down the slope and landed on the road in last winter's heavy rain is still a building site. Scaffolding planks, construction machinery, red-and-white plastic tape mark it off on the valley side. Severina has eyes for none of this. She stands by the grave, beside Massimo, with all the village people around them, behind them, filling the entire graveyard. Their eyes are not for the ornately adorned coffin but for Severina. She feels it. She dares not turn and look at anyone. She knows what is in their faces. That crazy mute who almost froze to death up there in winter with the old woman – who knows, Amabilia Brunetti might still be alive but for her. My God, the poor man. That is what their faces show, that is what they are thinking, so they aren't listening to Don Roberto but whispering, or exchanging meaningful glances.

Severina wants to push all this away from her, doesn't want to regret having come down. She did it for Massimo. And for herself, because she knew he wouldn't come back to her otherwise, and she couldn't live without him. Let them whisper and think and say what they please. Everything will get back to normal. Very surreptitiously, gently, her hand touches Massimo's. He looks at her, bewildered, and it seems to her as if he were smiling.

Later a strange party of mourners sits together in the little room above the Bar Sole. They are all mute, as if Severina's silence were a virus spreading round the table. What is one to say if she won't answer, what is one to ask? It's better to keep quiet, eat and drink, raise a glass to Massimo in silence and be glad that this means the wake will be a short one. Massimo sits at the head of the table, with Severina to his right and Rosanna to his left, as if she had equal rights. Rosanna says nothing either; it is as if talking were forbidden. Teresa's voice sounds all the louder as she and the young girl helping her bring in the separate courses and she announces them. It's often very merry at a wake, thinks Teresa. Too merry, so that you wouldn't believe the party was mourning a death. And quite often a wake degenerates into a loud, chaotic booze-up, with the heirs at daggers drawn, slagging off the dead person for making such a stupid will, and old ladies scurrying away while vigorously crossing themselves.

Down in the bar a couple of men are thinking their own thoughts about the silence up above.

That's how it ought to be when someone's died, says Teresa.

The men laugh.

Their laughter breaks into the middle of the decision Massimo has just made, with difficulty, to say something, at least to thank those present for coming to the funeral and for their condolences. But he says nothing, looks down the table, and his eyes linger on Anna, who is observing him with unconcealed avidity but a touch of derision too, an enigmatic smile behind the expression of sorrow she has assumed. And as usual when people keep silent instead of talking things over, everything that remains unsaid is out there in the open. You can see what people are thinking, and there's no chance of veiling it with fine words. So it would have been foolish to believe that Rosanna would fail to notice Anna's glances and her intentions, and see right through them.

Severina notices them too. Now, for the first time, she understands what it is like when other people keep silent. This is a new experience, for both the dead woman and Massimo always kept talking away at her own silence.

The only sounds are the clatter of the china, the chinking of knives, forks and spoons, the gurgling of bottles, sipping noises, the grinding of teeth, the cracking of poultry bones, the smacking of lips and several sighs, not quite stifled. And from below the men's laughter keeps echoing up to them. Is it mocking or comforting? Massimo doesn't know, and doesn't want to know.

Rosanna finds herself torn between hope and fear. Will Massimo really do as he said he would yesterday, when he needed her so much yet again? Will he stop going up the mountain if Severina won't speak? Will she speak? Will she come down from the loft and into the bedroom with him again? Or will she, Rosanna, be his lover for ever? The woman who could answer these questions sits there in silence, reading all Rosanna's thoughts in her flushed face.

Pressing her hand silently, Severina says goodbye outside Rosanna's house but does not go in. Instead, she starts up the path to the mountain without looking round again. Massimo stands there helplessly, watching Severina go, seeing that little gleam of triumph in Rosanna's eyes, and with a fleeting: See you soon, he sets out along the path himself. Tears rise to Rosanna's eyes, tears of fury and disappointment.

Severina does not have to look round. At first she senses that he is following her, then she hears him. Her own step is heavy, she's not used to walking this way any more. She stops on the little bridge over the brook, leans on the wooden balustrade, watches the water running by and sees Massimo, who is coming closer with powerful strides. It was here, twenty-one years ago, that he asked her if she would be his wife.

Will you?

I don't know – it's so sudden.

I've already spoken to your father.

You have?

Yes. He has no objection.

Are you sure he wasn't thinking of Anna?

No one mentioned any Anna.

Do you have to ask a girl's father first?

It's not compulsory.

Then he kissed her and hurried back to the village.

Then, in the past.

Now he is only a few steps away. Does a man like Massimo coming to this place remember what happened here too? No, thinks Severina, men forget such things.

He stands beside her and looks down at the water.

Do you have to ask a girl's father first?

You said.

My God, he does remember!

And what did I say then? Come on, tell me, what did I say?

She does not reply, but stands there before him.

Tell me!

She says nothing, rests her head on his chest, smells his sweat, the wine, the grappa, the incense.

It's not compulsory.

That's what I said.

He puts his arms round her. They stand like that for a few minutes, just as one can imagine they stood back then. Then they go on, hand in hand.

We've never done this in all our lives before.

Not even then.

Thinks Severina.

Massimo is silent too. Once they are up the mountain they change into their working clothes and go through the daily ritual of chores. Massimo feeds the rabbits and cleans out their hutch, puts grain in the bird-cage for the birds, mucks out the goats' shed and carries wood indoors. Severina lights the fire, fetches water from the spring and fills the kettle on the hearth. Then she goes up to the loft, fetches her bedclothes, the rifle, and everything else she has taken up there this year, and brings it all down. In the bedroom she puts clean sheets on the bed and replaces the wedding photograph on the bedside table. A glance out of the window shows her that Massimo is watching her and has understood what she is doing. He smiles, she sits down on the bed, stares at the floor, trembles in agitation.

Then they sit down at the table.

Massimo drinks wine, stares into the fire, avoids looking at her. While he used to keep talking as they sat here, perhaps to prove or explain something to his mother, now he is silent, as if telling Severina: Look, I can do it too, there's nothing to say or ask or explain now, it will be all right, I'm back, I'm here with you, and you know it, let's wait and see how things turn out.

Severina gets herself a glass too and pushes it over the table with a gesture of request. He takes the bottle and pours her a glass, surprised, because he can't remember ever seeing her drink wine before. They don't dare to clink glasses, they just raise them slightly, looking at each other for a split second, and then they drink. It is as if some of the eternal peace to which they committed the old woman's soul today has descended on the two of them as well.

They have never before sat alone at the table feeling like this.

Now he has really come back to me.

Thinks Severina.

They sit like that for a long time, silent, thinking their own thoughts.

Darkness falls outside.

They get up, go into the bedroom, undress in the dark, get into the bed on their usual sides and lie there quietly. Then one hand finds another, they move together, savouring every moment, every touch, the touches they haven't felt for so long, finding what is familiar again, discovering what is unknown.

Next morning they sit there as if feeling ashamed in front of each other. They crumble bread into their coffee, and gulp it down.

Can't you talk yet?

He asks.

She says nothing.

What do I have to do to make you talk?

She takes his hand, the rough, hairy, strong hand that she

felt on her body again in the night, and holds it tight, as if to say, give me time.

He sighs.

23

Why aren't human beings like marmots, thought Severina, as the winter went on far into February, with snowstorms and icy cold. If you were a marmot you could crawl into a cave in autumn, wind down all your thoughts and feelings, your heartbeat and pulse, your brain and your blood pressure to hibernation level, and sleep until the first rays of the sun woke you in March. Severina's strength was exhausted. So was the old woman's. She hardly ever spoke now. Several times, as she sat mute and motionless by the fire, Severina had to check that she was still alive. She would look up with wide, suffering eyes, as if to say: what have you done to me, what did you want, what was the idea, did you want me dead? But I haven't given you the satisfaction. I'm alive! I shall live until he comes back.

The winter was too harsh. It had come down over the mountains like an impenetrable shell, freezing all living things. The days were too short, the wish for light too great. The evenings and nights were too long. Severina had never liked winter. Even as a child she had been only half a human being for three months, a feebly flickering little light that would not catch fire from the Christmas candles and the crackling New Year bonfires, and found little comfort in those celebrations.

As if Nature meant to observe the calendar, winter ended on the first day of March. The first sunny days melted the snow and the first patches of green showed, as if splashed at random from a bucket of paint. The sheep raced happily out, chased around and welcomed the spring. And the old woman, still wrapped in a blanket, went to sit in her usual place on the bench outside the house, and immediately began to spend hours looking the way her son would be bound to come.

Severina was full of energy. She spring-cleaned, aired the place, did the laundry, cleared out the house and the yard, cleaned the stable, raked up the autumn leaves under the trees, took them to the compost heap, which had already thawed out, made all kinds of plans, decided to grow vegetables up here for the first time, wrote shopping lists for Franco-Francone, never rested, and was tired in the evenings. She felt like an animal waking from its long hibernation. She felt happy and confident, and could almost have sung out loud if she hadn't remembered her vow just in time. It did not escape her notice that the old woman disliked her cheerful mood, taking it as an indication that Severina was not missing her Massimo at all. But she was wrong. For with the animal spirits awakening in her, the desire for which there was scarcely room in her half-frozen heart during winter had returned. Severina kept catching herself looking into the distance too, looking the way from which he would first be seen coming.

Then someone appeared on the horizon. Severina recognised him at once from the way he walked: it was the faithful Franco-Francone, who had trudged up here several times in the winter to bring them the necessities of life. Once again he had a pannier full of provisions, which he spread out in front them. And he was very excited.

Massimo's coming!

He said.

He called Bruno, said he was coming. Yesterday or the day before, that was.

Excited as she was, Severina did not show it. All the life came back to the old woman's face. Franco-Francone repeated what he had said several times, so that they would be sure to believe him.

He's coming.

He really is coming.

By the Sacred Host, who'd have thought it!

Massimo is coming.

Say something, Severina!

Go on, say something!

You'll have to start talking when he comes back.

Severina looked at him, and gently passed her hand over his sweaty face.

Massimo did not arrive.

Instead, the men came up a week later: Franco-Francone, Bruno, Albino, Luigi and Paolo, a noisy, cheerful, inebriated party of hunters. They sat down in the yard, unpacked cheese, ham, bread and wine, ate and drank and talked.

Bruno never tired of deploring the fact that Massimo hadn't come back after all, and assuring everyone that Massimo really and truly had called his mobile when he, Bruno, and the other housepainters were renovating a villa belonging to a German Swiss.

This is Massimo.

He said.

Said Bruno.

Where are you?

I asked.

In Milan.

He said.

At the station.

He said.

I'm coming home by the next train.

He said.

Said Bruno.

I swear he said so.

I swear it.

Bruno repeated this and all the rest of it several times more, with increasing emphasis. They grew more relaxed, forgot about their hunt, went on drinking and finally started singing. The old woman sang happily along with them, croaking but in tune. She knew as well as Severina did that they all missed Massimo's voice. Not just his voice, they missed Massimo himself. But he was ever-present in the men's conversation, their reminiscences of the adventures they had had together. They too missed him, that was why they kept talking about him as if they could conjure him up, as if he would be there among them any moment now, clapping them on the shoulder, saying everything was all right again, asking: What's the matter, why don't you give us a song?

They sang, they ate and drank until well into the evening. Bruno took Severina's hand and danced to the men's singing with her, and there was a beautiful sparkle in his piggy eyes.

Say something, Severina.

Say something.

Anything.

We'll fetch him back if you just say the word.

We'll go to Milan. We'll find him and fetch him back.

But say something!

She kept silent, but she danced with him and enjoyed their company.

Lord, that Massimo!

Said Bruno.

I don't have a wife. Can't find one. No woman wants me. And there's Massimo, has a wonderful wife and goes away.

Leaves her alone. He's a bastard, is our friend Massimo, and a fool into the bargain.

No, he's not.

Said Franco-Francone.

The others just laughed.

Severina!

Said Bruno.

If he doesn't come back, take me! You don't have to talk as far as I'm concerned. I'd have you the way you are.

They made their noisy way down to the valley before it was dark.

The old woman had gone to bed long ago, and Severina sat on the bench outside the house for some time longer. She was shivering, for the evenings were still cold. But there was a starry sky above her such as you saw only up here. Happy, her feelings in turmoil, despairing yet nurturing a faint hope, doubting her vow yet firmly decided to keep it, she felt that life had returned. The last leaves of autumn fell from the trees, gleaming in the moonlight like shooting stars, and the peak of the Madonnina looked like some large, strange animal outlined against the moon.

Alessandro the joiner had never been up here before. Walking in the mountains was not in his style. But now he had brought with him his two sons Felice and Domenico, known as Mecco, and had set out to deal with one more piece of family business that couldn't be postponed any longer. It called for someone to put his foot down before it turned to tragedy.

He did not go into the house, didn't want any of the water or wine that the old woman offered him, or anything to eat.

Where is she?

He asked the old woman.

In the house, the stable, must be around somewhere.

Alessandro's sons found Severina behind the house, picking green stuff for the rabbits.

Can't you come and say hello to your father?

Said Alessandro.

She said nothing, but nodded to her brothers and to her father too.

Aren't you talking yet?

She shook her head.

You'll have to start talking some time.

Where is he? Have you heard anything from him?

Tell us!

Open your mouth and tell us!

Shouted Mecco.

When your father asks you a question!

Added Felice.

So you don't know anything? You haven't heard anything?

She shook her head.

We'll damn well make you talk!

Shouted Felice, grabbing her and shaking her.

She did not scream, she did not weep. He hit out at her. Then their father came between them, slinging his son away.

You will not beat your sister! It's someone else who deserves a beating, and we're going to look for him. And we'll find him! And when we bring him back here you'll be kind enough to talk!

She looked sadly at him. She had no means of conveying anything to him. But, she thought, if you do something to a person that you never did before, perhaps then he'll understand you. So she went up to him, hugged him, and kissed him on both cheeks. He stood there stiffly, letting her do it, then he turned, called his sons in as you might whistle back two hunting hounds who have just set off to pursue the trail of some animal, and went away. Severina watched him go with tears in her eyes. And suddenly, after all these years, she longed for the first time for her parental home, for the kitchen where he usually sat alone, for the little garden behind the house, for the smell of the joiner's workshop which was lingering in his clothes just now when she embraced him.

24

Autumn is coming, and it is getting colder up here. In a few weeks it will be time to go down to the village. And Severina is still mute. Massimo has tried everything. He has shouted at her, given her a fright, woken her abruptly in the middle of the night to ask sudden questions. He even remained silent himself for days, and found it so difficult that he can't understand anyone voluntarily doing such a thing. He almost admires her. And when he lies beside her and touches her, and she isn't just putting up with it but enjoying it, he whispers in her ear that he will be patient and wait until she has words for him again, if he can only lie with her like this. But then the fury comes back, desperation seizes on him, he has to be with people who talk. He accepts work that will bring him into the company of other people. He chops wood with Franco-Francone and drives it to the pizzerias beside the lake with Albino. He stays down in the village for days. And inevitably he meets Anna again, and she tries to entice him, but he will not respond to her courtship of him, he is afraid of the problems. Anna would be triumphant, would do everything she could to make sure Severina heard of it. And people would talk about it in the village, out loud, even the mute woman up on the mountain couldn't help hearing it. In the evenings Massimo goes round the villages with his friends, is seen in all the bars, is often the centre of merry drinking sessions. No one asks after Severina any more. He is back, that's what matters, the valleys have him back again. And as if he had to prove something to them, polishing up his old reputation, one day when they are chopping wood up in the forest he soars over the valley on a load of timber yet again. Of course people talk about that, more than they talk about the fact that he went away for a year but has come back to his wife, who has lost the power of speech – poor man, they say, even the women.

The affair with Teresa has remained, as she decided it should, a one-night stand. She has kept it to herself, which might well be considered a miracle, hasn't even crowed over Rosanna, who now greatly enjoys winning back her lover from Teresa.

Teresa knows that she couldn't live with a long-term relationship like that, not here, not running the bar. So she and Massimo keep their secret. No one notices anything, and yet their behaviour to each other is different. Sometimes they suddenly glance at one another and smile in the course of an evening. Massimo would not be the man he is if he didn't think, secretly, that the episode might be repeated. But not now, when his life isn't back to normal yet, when he has returned to everyone else but not yet to Severina, not really, or else she hasn't returned to him, since she still won't speak.

The bar fills up very quickly with men from the village in a state of great excitement. They are shouting confusedly at each other, ranting, gesticulating, indignant, up in arms. It seems that they feel their own honour, the honour of their wives and the honour of their native land have all been deeply injured.

What's happened?

Asks Massimo.

They are all talking at once, and it turns out that there was a Japanese on today's Saturday evening TV show making spaghetti out of dough with his bare hands, fine spaghetti, nothing the matter with that spaghetti in itself. There he stood with his legs apart like a conjuror, as if making spaghetti was magic, floured his hands, picked up the dough, stretched it out with his arms spread wide, folded it in half and stretched it out again. The rope of dough became thinner and thinner, he threw flour in the air again and rolled the strings of dough in it, for by now he had formed it into several strings. He stretched them out, the strings became thinner and thinner, in the end they were just threads, threads stretched between his outspread arms as he passed them from hand to hand. And after a few minutes, would you believe your eyes, he had trimmed the ends and thrown a pile of the best, most perfect spaghetti on a large dish that some women brought in. To cap it all, they had been playing dramatic music, as if making spaghetti was a great drama, as if you needed musical accompaniment. And the audience clapped as if they'd never in their lives seen spaghetti made before.

And they show that kind of thing on TV.

What shit!

I switched over.

They show our wives a programme like that.

And our wives watch it too!

I switched right off.

Wouldn't have anything to do with it.

Since when can the Japanese make spaghetti?

Asks Bruno.

Who knows what it tastes like?

I mean, okay, let the Japanese make spaghetti.

But why do they have to show it on TV?

It's an insult.

To our wives.

An insult to my wife's spaghetti.

Shouts Albino.

Well, I don't know, your wife's spaghetti...
Says Franco-Francone.
Do you have anything against my wife's spaghetti?
My Anna makes the best spaghetti in the world.
I never eat anything but Mirella's spaghetti.
And they show a programme like that on TV.
I'm not switching on again.
And the women watch it, too.
It's an insult.
A Japanese, of all things!
Standing there.
Legs apart.
Giancarlo imitates him.
That's how he was standing.
Throwing flour in the air.
Just imagine my Grazia standing in the kitchen.
Legs apart.
Throwing flour in the air!
Stretching the dough out like that.
I can just see it!
Says Bruno.
The Japanese, of all people.
All those Asiatics.
On TV too.
The hell with the lot of them.
Did you hear about Antonio?
Asks Bruno.
Which Antonio?
Antonio from the market.
Who sells shirts and jackets.
Antonio from Grandola.
What about Antonio?
He shot the pharmacist's dog. The pharmacist from Osteno.

What for?

His wife had been having it off with the pharmacist from Osteno.

So he shot the dog.

Why the dog?

Because the pharmacist wasn't at home.

They talk on, thinking up various methods of torture and execution suitable for the Japanese, the television company, the pharmacist from Osteno and Antonio's wife. They are even prepared to feel sorry for the pharmacist's dog, who died but was, after all, perfectly innocent. Massimo feels strange that evening. He listens to the conversations but takes no part in them, he watches the card-players but does not follow their game, he looks at Teresa and right through her. He is thinking, and this surprises him, of Severina. Again and again, more and more intensely. He sees her sitting at the table, leafing through the magazines he always has to bring up from Tiziana's shop, sighing over all the nonsense in the world. Now that she doesn't even have his mother to quarrel with she is very much alone through the long days, the long nights. Perhaps he should take her up a little television set some time. Or a mobile like Bruno's. But who would she call? He could call her. Oh God, no, she isn't talking. He'd be calling to tell her when he was coming back, say he wouldn't be back today but he'd be there tomorrow, and she wouldn't answer. Doesn't she talk even when she's on her own? She always used to pray out loud, or at least audibly, reciting long rosaries. He can't imagine her praying in silence. He knows no woman who can do that. They'd feel as if they were cheating God. Men do it, they fold their hands and pray in silence. Or no, they don't really pray, they're thinking of something totally different, that last game of bowls, or the partridge they shot yesterday, their cars or a woman they fancy. As a child, whenever they said prayers at home or at church or beside a grave, he always used to think of naked women, in so far as he knew at the time what naked women looked like, just to annoy God.

Surely she talks when she's on her own. Perhaps she curses and swears at him, perhaps she says all the things she'd like to say to him if she hadn't made that vow never to speak again to the man who deserted her so shamefully. For he did desert her shamefully, he knows it. They've told him, Teresa and Rosanna and other people too, how she went all round the village calling his name, how she visited the carabinieri, and he has seen for himself the way she took out her fury on the house. Would other women do that if their husbands left? He can't think of one who would. Luisa might. She'd go crazy. Has Severina gone crazy? Is her silence a sign of madness? Will she never speak again? Should he consult the doctor some time?

Massimo desires Severina. It's a feeling he had forgotten. When he desired something in Milan it wasn't her, or not just her, it was the valleys, the village, the mountain, the farmyard and the animals, the people, the bar, the cables crossing the ravines. He had felt that in the city you are nobody, nothing, but here in the valleys I am Massimo the eagle, someone they know, the man who flew over the ravine, over the valley. It was a desire to be the man he once was again. But now he desires Severina. He sees her before him, wearily putting the magazines down, getting to her feet, rubbing her aching back, going out again to make sure the stable door is closed, coming in, washing herself at the sink, going into the bedroom, not up to the loft any more, taking her clothes off, putting on her long night-dress, lying down with a sigh, praying, falling asleep. He would like to be lying beside her now, feeling her warm, plump body, hearing her regular breathing, her tiny snores now and then. And she would show him that she wasn't quite asleep, and he would say, just think, they showed a Japanese on TV making spaghetti with his bare hands. And she would laugh! Yes, she'd laugh! Wouldn't audible laughter be almost as good as speaking? She hasn't laughed yet since he came back, not even soundlessly. She has made love in silence too.

Massimo leaves the bar with the last of the men, and Teresa closes up behind them. When they have relieved themselves against the wall of the square one last time, still cursing the Japanese, they go home.

It is a clear night. There are as many stars in the sky as there are thoughts in Massimo's head. His feelings are churned up. Something must change. She must speak. She must speak because she wants to, because he's with her and she never again has to be afraid that he will go away a second time, because he has shown her that he is hers. Because he loves her.

He must go up there now. He won't go to see Rosanna, who even in bed keeps on showing him that, unlike his wife, she is well able to talk, when it would be better if she simply kept quiet for once instead of describing and explaining everything, rabbiting on and on about it. No, he ought not to go to see Rosanna now. Or Teresa either.

And he won't go to see Anna either, he will not fall into the dangerous spider's web she has spun. No, he will go up the mountain. Lie down with Severina, hold her tight, be with her. He sets out.

He recently saw two young people, a couple of lovers, sitting on the little bench outside the Bar Sole, holding hands, looking into each other's eyes, kissing, and they both said, at the same time:

I love you.

Massimo had not been mistaken, he was standing close, surreptitiously watching the two of them, and he heard it clearly.

I love you.

They said to each other.

Massimo can't remember ever in his life having said *I love you* to anyone. Even when he fell in love with Severina in Oggia he didn't say it, nor did he say it later, or to Renata either.

When he gets into bed beside Severina an hour later, nestling against her back, feeling her gentle, regular breathing, he says: There was a Japanese making spaghetti on TV. Silence, she seems to be asleep. He strokes her neck, turns over on his back, looks at the ceiling.

I love you.

He says.

While they are drinking their coffee next morning, dipping bread in it, sitting there in silence, and fury threatens to rise in Massimo again because of that leaden silence, Severina suddenly laughs. She laughs! She actually laughs. Audibly, out loud, her laughter echoing round the kitchen, out to the sheep in their pasture, out to the birds in the trees.

What are you laughing at?

A Japanese, making spaghetti!

She says.

She says!

They are both startled, and stare at each other. Severina, horrified, puts her hand over her mouth, as if she could fetch back the words that came out of it.

You spoke – you – you said something – Good Lord in Heaven, you spoke!

She does not reply.

Talk to me! Say something, anything, go on talking, please say something!

What? I don't know – what shall I say?

Anything, everything that comes into your mind, laugh, sing, pray, yes, pray, Severina, say an Our Father or a rosary.

She begins to pray.

Our Father.

And she prays and prays and prays. Massimo is beside himself with joy, entranced, crazy with delight. He runs out and shouts up to the peak of the Madonnina: She's talking! He goes back in, gets down at her feet, weeps for joy, puts his head on her lap.

And she prays all the verses of the rosary, Hail Mary full of grace, and then an Our Father, over and over again.

You're talking! Listen, will you, you're talking!

Blessed art thou among women, and blessed is the fruit of thy womb.

He has to tell people, let everyone know, shout it out loud: She's talking. She's a human being again, his wife to whom he has returned. She's talking!

He goes down in haste, running. He wishes he could fly.

He arrives in the bar drenched in sweat and exhausted, breathing heavily, stands there as if he had seen the Devil himself, stares at Teresa and the card-players and the young men at the bar.

She's talking!

He says.

A short silence, they look at each other, then at him, they see he expects some reaction, enthusiasm, maybe delight.

Franco-Francone takes pity on him.

It's miracle. Thanks be to the Lord.

Yes, a miracle.

What's she saying, then?

She's praying.

She's praying?

She's praying.

And he is gone again. Silence in the room, as if someone had just brought news of a death and none of them could take it in.

She's praying!

Says Luigi in a fluting voice, and he laughs. But not for long, because he thinks of his Luisa at home, and the way she can't get the skeleton in the yellow jacket out of her head, and how it has made her mute. Oh, if only she would speak again, talk nonsense to him the way she used to! Luisa, thinks Luigi, Luisa doesn't even pray any more.

Poor Massimo.

Says Albino.

Now she's gone crazy.

Says Bruno.

Now everything is back to normal.

Says Teresa.

And she smiles as she says it.

25

They were coming down from the peak of the Madonnina mountain, without seeing the Madonnina herself. There was mist and fog up there, they hadn't seen the statue. They hadn't seen anything, as Massimo, who is familiar with the weather here, had known in advance. But they refused to believe him. And after all, she was there, the burden he carried up and down. A burden lighter than the fully-laden pannier that he used to carry up from the valley. Down they came, the young men bad-tempered, scratched, their feet blistered, their trousers torn, their shoes battered. They had stumbled, fallen and slid. Their elbows, knees and hands were scraped. Their equipment had not been up to a climb to the peak of the Madonnina, and they were cursing and swearing. They'd seen none of what everyone, they said, had promised them down in the bar. Everyone, said Massimo, but not me. They hadn't seen a thing, not a trace of the bloody Madonnina. The young men lay down in the grass, leaned against trees, demanded food and drink, or drink anyway, and licked their wounds. Massimo brought them what they had in the house, went to fetch wine, brought out some bread, sliced ham and salami. He glanced surreptitiously at Severina. At first she stayed indoors. Perhaps she noticed what he himself had realised, before the wine took his mind off it: he wasn't doing it for these four wind-blown scarecrows, only for the woman, who finally put a stop to her companions' whining. They'd wanted a good time, she said, and they were having a good time, anyone who wasn't having a good time could go down again, there was the path. She wanted a good time and she was having it. What more could you wish for than wine and bread, cheese and ham, and such a generous host? She jumped up at Massimo, who didn't know what had come over him, who was still holding back so as not to hurt Severina, she wound her arms round his neck and her legs round his hips and kissed him on the mouth. I wouldn't mind more of that, he thought. He glanced very briefly at the house, saw Severina going into the shed, turned Renata round to hold her a little way from him, her feet touching the ground again, and within a second it looked as if she had just been leaning on him for a moment so as not to fall. She acknowledged this with a peal of laughter that showed her crooked incisors, which had appealed to Massimo from the first. Severina disappeared into the shed. She seemed not to want to see what she guessed at, what Massimo knew already: he was lost, if he had ever resisted at all he had given up resisting now, something bound to happen was indeed happening to him. Renata was using him, sucking him dry, driving the sense out of his brain and the blood to his head. He gave himself up to her, and that made her crazy for it. She wanted more from him. She wanted the whole man, a man who in her eyes might have been carved from wood, strange, charming, strong. Even the old woman, his mother, watched in surprise from the bench outside the house; she had never seen her son like this, her beloved son who always did everything right, her only son who, as she always thought, was certainly different from other people, often more daring, more determined, admired by so many, envied too. He had chosen to marry this Severina, something she had not been able to understand at all, for any woman would have wanted him, women who were prettier, richer, livelier than the one he had chosen, preferring her to her sister. Now the old woman sent a couple of sighs up to heaven. What was he doing? What was happening to him? She, who liked to join in with her croaking old woman's voice when, with rapt attention, he sang the familiar part-songs with the other men, all standing correctly upright, was silent now that he was giving the songs away to these strangers. She said nothing, but a vague anxiety took hold of her, the anxiety she had always felt when he was a child and wanted to be different from other children. Now she feared that something might change, he might leave her and Severina, leave the two of them alone up here, and that would not be good, since there had been a gulf between the two women from the first, involving them in a power struggle that she kept inflaming by interfering in a small way, with doubts, digs and gibes at her daughter-in-law. Would what was going on now have been possible if they'd had more children after the baby who died so young? Would he abandon a son? She said nothing, stared at the scene, saw Severina retreat from the visitors as Massimo advanced towards them.

He sang, laughed, drank, was quite beside himself, danced himself into another world, and felt that he was lost to his life up here. Intoxication made him careless. All this would lead somewhere, down to the valley, perhaps to Teresa's bar. Tomorrow was another day. He was dangling from the cable again with a storm coming up, he was flying, flying like the birds over the little valleys, the hills, the Alpine meadows, the houses and huts, over the deserted village of Oggia, flying away somewhere, anywhere. He was flying, and everyone could see him!

26

Snow has fallen overnight. The peak of the Madonnina, powdered as if with white sugar, rises into the blue sky, a pale, ghostly finger, far away all of a sudden, apparently unconquerable, forbidding. It has grown cold. The snow will settle up here. Winter has come to the mountains even earlier than last year, as if telling them it is time to leave. Even the silvery trees seem to be freezing. There is something unapproachable about them now, they want to be alone with the coming winter.

Massimo secures the firewood and locks it up, clears tools into the shed, kills the two rabbits he can't take down to the valley alive, drives the goats and sheep together in the farmyard. They are now looking around, agitated, and nibbling the last sparse blades of grass at the sides of the yard and under the trees, bleating expectantly as they wait for what the older animals among them already anticipate, the climb down to the valley, the warmer stables there, the fresh hay, the different sounds that will reach their ears.

Severina has cleaned the hearth, swept the kitchen and the bedroom, tidied up, packed the last of the food into a pannier, stripped the bed, put the sheets on top of the pannier and wrapped the wedding photograph in them. She handled it almost tenderly, because now it has a meaning for her again.

Soon it will be quiet up here. The trees will fall into their own kind of half-wakeful hibernation, lose their last, stiffly frozen leaves, let their sap sink towards the ground and defy the cold winds.

In silence, Severina and Massimo carry out their usual tasks, a familiar way of life only briefly interrupted, now won back. They do not have to talk. They are still spellbound by the peace they have made with each other, their return to living life together, and they both feel that they have warmth to fight off the cold coming down over the countryside. For he has come home! What they feel now they will never say to each other, for they have never said such things, they have had no words for them, let alone grand words. In her unhappiness Severina did not speak at all. Massimo did speak in his unhappiness, which he took for happiness, and now that he has made her speak again they can both be silent.

A small procession, a caravan, they move away from the farm. The animals go in front, those who know the way leading the young ones, Massimo behind them, laden with everything they don't want to leave up here, after him Severina with the pannier, which is also loaded to the brim.

He has come back, he has come back to her, he has taken his place beside her again! This thought keeps going through Severina's head. Even now, when she sees his sturdy figure ahead of her, the pannier on his back with the two skinned, half-frozen rabbits dangling from it, and she has difficulty keeping up with him, she is full of warmth to know that he is there and gives herself up to that happy feeling, a secret little extravagance of her heart, her heart that was afraid for so long. It's the extravagant feeling you can have only in times of good fortune, a belief that she really never doubted he would come back. She is full of hope, pride and confidence. She doesn't know if she could have spent another winter up here, if she'd have had the strength for it. She doesn't even know exactly where she found the strength to get through the last one. It can't have come solely from sadness, despair and loneliness. It must, after all, have been this certainty of hers, something she hardly admitted to herself, a little light warming her in the darkness of winter.

To Massimo, striding powerfully along, repeatedly driving the animals back to the path when they stray too far from it, the world is back on course again. It has to be the way it is now. It ought always to have been that way, it never ought to have changed, for it had been so good over the years. He knows she is behind him, hears her footsteps, her gasping for air, thinks he can feel her breath, her body, her warmth, all the happiness of his return, that confidence, that sense of coming home described by the old men who had been away a long time in the war. Massimo knows it is not a good idea to leave this place, not for any reason at all. So why did he do it? What was it? What made him risk his whole life in pursuit of that fluttering bird? Was it like a little boy jumping a brook, with the chance of either falling in the water or landing safely on the opposite bank? Was it the idea of something strange and alien, experience that he ought not to be living or to have lived through, but which he has always secretly sought because what is known, familiar, liveable had become tedious, taken too much for granted? Was it what people call adventure when they read about it, with bated breath, in children's books or see it later on television, another world? Was it his wish to fly, his dream since childhood, the feeling he had when he hitched himself to that load of timber as the storm rose, and soared over the valley to the opposite hill and down to the village, staking his life, aware of the deadly danger below? No one else here had ever done that before. At the time he had a sense of unbounded power and superiority. He was a superman, flying over the valley like a bird. It was a victory over his own fear. And he was sure of admiration. Did he think that if he did extraordinary things in his own world, nothing could harm him in that other world which itself was extraordinary? Or was it really just the woman, that exotic bird? Was it the crooked front teeth she showed when she laughed, her green eyes, her small breasts, the intoxicating fragrance of sweat and perfume around her, her hot breath on his neck when he carried her up to the peak of the Madonnina and then down again, the soft, gentle hands that she pushed inside his shirt? Certainly all those things made him go. And it was the many nights in her bed that made him stay, nights that beguiled him before they gave way to humiliation and angry words. Whether he wants to or not, he keeps thinking of the delicate, fragile, bird-like body for which he had betrayed his previous life. What would have happened if she hadn't changed so much? Would there have been any awakening, would he have thought better of it and wanted to go home? Could Alessandro have done anything then? Would he be walking down to the valley in front of Severina now, with a laden pannier on his back, looking forward to a warm winter down in the village? He dares not pursue these thoughts. Thinking can be dangerous.

The snow shows them the way they are going. Severina tries to tread in Massimo's footsteps. As a child she always did that when she walked behind her father in winter. She had to jump to keep in his tracks then, and even now she can't keep pace with Massimo for long.

There he is. He has come home! Does he still think of that woman? Will anything like it happen to him again? Severina does not think that thought to the end. She wants to forgive and forget, above all to forget. She wants to show him that she has forgotten. She doesn't know what it will be like down in the village. She wants to shout out to all of them down there: He's back!

Yes, she will forget. Time will be merciful, will blur the traces until they are unrecognisable.

But Severina will never again forget that face. A face in which all the malice and stupidity, all the arrogance and presumption of which a human being is capable are united. The face of the young carabinieri Adriano Rossi at the police station down in the valley.